REGINE

or *Love In The Antilles*

by E.K.

&

THE PANGS OF VENUS

Anonymous

A STAR BOOK
published by
the Paperback Division of
W.H. Allen & Co. PLC

A Star Book
Published in 1987
by the Paperback Division of
W.H.Allen & Co. PLC
44 Hill Street, London W1X 8LB

Printed and bound in Great Britain by
Anchor Brendon Ltd, Tiptree, Essex

ISBN 0 352 31872 4

REGINE

"At last," I cried, "here is a tree that is easy to climb and loaded with fruit." I got up on one of the lowest branches. "I'll pick the mangoes, Monsieur Martel, and throw them down to you."

He took up his post while I climbed above his head. I noted that his eyes were following me. Suddenly, there popped into my head the thought that this was the ideal occasion to give him a glimpse of my secret charms.

I scrambled from branch to branch. It was a sweltering hot day, and I was not wearing any underpants. Also my petticoat was very short. Slyly looking at him below, I could make out that his face had turned scarlet and that his eyes were glittering with an unaccustomed fire . . .

REGINE

or *Love In The Antilles*

by E.K.

Translated from the French by Howard Nelson

BOOK I

CHAPTER I

MY PARENTS AND
MY GIRLHOOD

Before the emancipation of the slaves, my father, who was of English origin, owned vast and rich plantations in the Antilles. It was on one of them that I was born. At my baptism, I was given the name of Regine.

I do not believe that my readers will be interested in my infancy with such details as my first tooth and my childhood diseases. The first event that pertains to my subject occurred when I was sixteen years old, and I remember it as if it were yesterday.

At that time, I was given to the care of a Negress named Dora whose sole task was to look after me. Through her, I learned that my mother who died shortly after giving me birth was nothing but a favourite slave. It seems that she was a rare beauty with a complexion almost as white as that of a European woman. Dora told me that I looked very much like her.

I should mention that my nurse was very learned in herbs. She boasted that with her knowledge, she could cure any ailment known to man.

One herb that she often picked during our strolls she used in place of tea. It also possessed soporific powers. I remember always falling into a delicious sleep right after she gave me a cup of the brew.

One evening, she prepared the beverage, but I noticed it had a more penetrating odour than usual. Perhaps because of my stomach, it had a disagreeable taste. When she was not looking, I started to empty the contents of the cup in a flower pot, but she caught me. At her insistence, I did manage to get a few drops down.

The need I had for sleep undoubtedly came from the brew, but it seemed weaker for I woke up after only a few hours. Moonbeams were shining through the curtain into my room. By their light, I was able to make out the clock face. It was just a little after midnight.

I felt nervous and feverish. I put my hand on my cunt. I found the two lips and the satiny *mons veneris*. With my finger, I gently rubbed the crevice that separated them. I could smell a delightful scent emanating from it. I felt it half open under my fondling. It seemed to me that this organ I had just discovered was intimately and mysteriously bound to my life, to the very source of my being. At that time, I was ignorant of the marvellous key which, when inserted, starts the mysterious action.

But now that the veil had been partially lifted, my curiosity was all the more whetted. Also, many things I had only guessed at before became clearer. I made up my mind to find all I could about the subject.

I was lying in bed, wrapped up in those thoughts, when a low whistle caught my attention. Dora also had heard it, for she quickly got up and whispered: "Is that you, Dandy?"

The whistle was repeated.

"It's all right for you to come in," she said. "The child is dead to the world."

A dark form appeared at the window. I recognised him. He was an overseer, a good-looking mulatto who was known to be a passionate admirer of Dora. He took her in his arms and gave her a long kiss.

"Are you sure the girl is sound asleep? I'd like to take a look at that little cunt of hers," he said.

"Of course she's asleep. My herb tea never fails."

Walking on tiptoe, the mulatto approached my bed. Gently he lifted the sheets and slipped his hand between my thighs. I pretended that I was asleep, although I found it hard to remain motionless. His fingers were tickling me. Soon I experienced that pleasure I had before. For fear that the delightful sensation would stop, I kept myself rigid as a rock.

"What an adorable little cunt she has," he commented. "Do you know, Dora, I'd like to be the first to pluck that enticing flower."

"Hee, hee!" she laughed. "I wouldn't be surprised if her father is going to have the honour. You don't know what she told me."

"Well, that doesn't surprise me. Everyone knows what a skirt chaser he is. Does he have you often, Dora?" he asked.

"Oh, he comes now and then when he gets the notion that he would like to play around with a black cunt."

"Do you give him all he wants?"

"Why not?" She shrugged her shoulders as she fondled the scarlet tip of the tool with the large round head that she had pulled out of his pants. With one hand, she seemed to be holding up while with the other she was agitating up and down the big ebony member.

Now he came back to me. Because of his titillations, the mulatto had brought my slit to such a state of excitation that he was able to insert the tip of his finger into the tight entrance. The pain, however, was so great that I bit my lips together to keep my screams back. Nevertheless, the sensation that I was undergoing was so nerve-wracking that when Dandy tried to get his finger in all the way, I gave such a convulsive movement that, all of a sudden, I felt something break within me. From that moment, to my great relief, he could push his finger in and out of me without my feeling any pain.

"I am positive that she is on the point of being able to be plucked," Dandy exclaimed, "even though she does not have any hair yet on her mound. Look, Dora, my finger has gone into the bottom, and she doesn't even awake."

"Yes, I see, but don't go too far with her. Come on, let me finish you off, after which you will go off to bed like a good boy."

Saying that, she took him by his peg and pulled him to the bed. There she sat, imprisoning the bone between her legs. Passing his hand between her thighs, he threw her on her back. Then she spread her legs open like a wide book, revealing to my eyes her enormous cavern.

The contours of her lips, thick and fat, were of a swarthy colour, while the interior was of a bright red and seemed to be overflowing with an oily liquid.

"Let me put it in, Dandy," she said as she clutched the organ which she guided to the immense aperture like a ravenous creature.

"Push, push, you rascal," she cried while she dug her fingernails into the quivering flesh of his buttocks. "Go to it. Get your wonderful prick to the very bottom. Fuck me like the man you are!"

Enthusiastic about his task, Dandy lost no time in obeying her injunctions. He was pumping with such verve that the whole room shook from his vigorous jabs. Once his chore was terminated, he fell in a semi-faint on my nurses's body, got up, and left.

The events of that night completely changed my existence. I did not remain innocent for long. New sensations had been born in me. I had felt a sharp desire for something . . . but what? I now had a glimmering what it is between a man and woman and I wanted it.

I had a tutor who was teaching me how to read and write. I loved to read, but there were not many books at my disposition. The few I could find were mostly poets like Byron, Burns, and Keats. Today, I constantly reread them, always with increasing interest. Always they have the power to stimulate my jaded tastes.

My mind in those days, however, was inclined to study the things with which I was in daily contact and to analyse the events which took place around me, particularly those occurrences which sharpened my already lively curiosity.

I began life in an atmosphere corrupted by sensuality. I am astonished that I was able to remain so long untouched in such a milieu. My father was a man of robust health and unbridled passions. He enjoyed unlimited power over a number of women

13

of all stations and temperaments. Since he was good-hearted and generous, and handsome, to boot, women were more than eager to satisfy his every wish, no matter what it might be. He was far from being selfish in his pleasures, leaving his supervisors and overseers, many of whom were European, the same liberty he claimed for himself. In other words, there reigned on the plantation an unbridled promiscuity and a disgraceful licence.

One of the sons of the head supervisor was allowed to share in my games during the hours he was free. His name was Dick and he was about my age. On more than one occassion, he attempted to take liberties with me. Up to then, I had always repulsed his advances, but after what I had witnessed, I decided to allow him to go a little further.

When he returned to play with me, he recommenced his usual tricks, most of which consisted in trying to put his hand up my skirt.

"Oh, Dick, why can't you keep your hands where they belong?" I protested. "What do you think I have down there, a pocket full of nuts and bonbons?"

"No. You have there a very lovely flower that I would give anything to look at and then pluck."

"What silly things you are saying. How can you know if I have a blossom there or any other thing?"

"I know very well, and you don't have to get upset about it," he declared. "I got a look at my sister when she was taking her bath, I peeked and saw that she had between her legs the loveliest little mouth imaginable."

"And what do you have in that same place?" I inquired.

"I'll show it to you," as he undid his trousers. "Ah, there it is. Wouldn't you like to take it in your hand?"

"I'd never touch a dirty little thing like that!" I exclaimed in mock horror. But I could not keep my eyes from it.

"Why do you call it a dirty little thing, Regine, when you know you think just the contrary. Just look how proud it is and how it stands up!" He then pulled down the skin covering the extremity. "There. Look how he is showing you the tip of his nose. Tell me if you know what that is made for, Regine."

"Of course not. How should I know anything about any object like that?"

"I bet you know more than you let on. Well, I'll tell you anyhow. This pretty little toy has been fashioned just to penetrate that pretty hole you have between your legs. Be nice and let me touch it."

After much laughing, rebuffs, and little shoves, he succeeded in slipping his hand into my little valley of delights. I was happy to see how his handsome face beamed when he felt under his agile fingers the soft contours and the rounded velvet of the lips forming the outer part of my little fleeceless organ. He hugged and kissed me with all his might as he attempted to lay me on my back and get his legs between mine. Pinching my clitoris, he slipped his fingers in my slit. Finally, he managed to get up my skirt and opened my panties so wide that I ended by yielding and granting him what he so ardently desired—the unencumbered view of my rose crevice.

How his eyes glittered! How he rained kisses on those desirable lips! With what ardour he darted

15

his whole tongue into my little cunt. He was bent over me, my hand was supporting his thigh, and his trousers were open.

When I clutched his prick, it haughtily stood at attention as soon as my fingers were wrapped around it. That seemed to give him an enormous pleasure. He pushed me back a little so he could make another inspection. He taught me how to masturbate him, as he called revealing and concealing the gland's head. With the greatest satisfaction, he contemplated the operation.

Gradually, he had brought his prick to my lips. Now he asked me to kiss it. Then he put the head between my lips and tickled my nose. It had a particular smell and odour, which pleased and excited me.

Acceding to his pleas, I ended up by taking the whole thing in my mouth and rolling my tongue around it. Then he made me fondle his testicles, after which he guided my fingers until they reached the little orifice of his backside.

In spite of his age, Dick was a true gentleman and did his part in our games.

"Darling," he said, "you are an incomparable treasure. You know how to bestow pleasure on a man and you have a jewel of a cunt. For the time, let's keep this between ourselves, and in the meantime, I'll teach you many new things. How is that?"

"Oh, Dick, I gladly agree. You are a good fellow. Really, I love you and I want to seal our pact with a kiss."

"Regine, you will be my only love!" he assured me earnestly. "I'll marry you as soon as I have made a start in life. But, tell me, do you know the name of what you are holding in your hand and that you are kneading so gently?"

"Indeed, Dick, I have to admit my ignorance."

"It's a prick; what you have is called a cunt," he informed me. "When you insert the prick into the cunt, it is the most wonderful sensation you can imagine. That's known as fucking. There are many other names for these three words, but you'll learn them as we go along, so I won't bother taking the time now. Now on your back, my dear, and spread open your thighs as wide as you can. Still more if you can. Now we are going to fuck. If I can get my prick into your divine cunt, you will learn the incomparable pleasures of this form of love-making."

Stretching out on my back and opening my legs, I tried to spread open my cunt with my fingers. At the same time, Dick was kneeling between my thighs and placing the head of his gland against my aperture. He pushed forward. I helped all I could, but unfortunately, our efforts were in vain. He was unable to penetrate.

At the end, a jewel of whitish liquor escaped from his prick. With a comic look of despair at his lack of success, he got up from me. Feeling sorry for him, I asked: "But Dick, how do you know it is supposed to go in there?"

"I have seen it done many times. Do you want me to tell you what I saw just last week?"

"Yes, go ahead," I told him. "I'm all ears."

"Regine, you don't know about old Snigger who has the cat-o'-nine-tails; it is his job to whip the slaves that get out of line. They are sent to him with a note from my father. Last week, our maid Sally was both lazy and sassy, and my father made

17

up his mind to teach her a good lesson by turning her over to Snigger. He wrote a note along these lines: 'Administer to the girl bringing you this word a good dozen lashes to teach her how to behave herself.' Sally did as she was told and brought it.

"Having a good idea of the contents of the letter, I thought I knew where she was going, so I followed her. I hid behind the shed where all the punishments are carried out in a spot where I could see everything that was going to take place.

"The old man made her come in and locked the door after her.

"When the poor girl realised what was in store for her, she was frozen with fright and began to weep.

" 'Come, come,' said Snigger, trying to console her. 'If you are nice and gentle, I won't hurt you very much.'

"He tied her hands together and placed her on a bench so that her derriere was stuck up in the air. Then he pulled her dress over her head and placing his hand between the girl's yellow legs, he forced them wide apart. Breaking into tears again, she began to call him names.

" 'So that's how you are,' Mr Snigger observed. 'Since you don't want to be quiet, I guess you have to take what is coming to you.'

"With that, he made the whip whistle in the air and let it fall with a crack on the tenderest part of her chubby flesh.

"She twitched and gave out a piercing scream.

" 'Wonderful!' remarked the old man, letting the strands drop again with a resounding report. 'Perhaps now you will be reasonable and let yourself be given clemency.'

" 'Oh, yes Mr Snigger,' she snivelled. 'I'll be as good as I can. But for heavens sake, don't hit me again, please, for it hurts like anything.'

" 'I don't want to flog you at all, Sally,' replied the withered monkey, running his hands over her thick thighs, spreading them apart, and regarding avidly the gaping aperture.

"Letting his trousers fall, you would have been amazed at its size. He rubbed it until it stiffened in his hand, and then seizing the girl by her haunches, he brutally shoved his prick into the cunt. She protested violently, saying that such was not one of his functions, when she felt his gland against her grotto.

" 'Do you want to feel the cat again?' he said menacingly, giving her a gentle tap.

" 'Oh, Mr Snigger, don't hit me again! You can do anything you want to me as long as you don't strike me again.'

" 'Now you're being a sensible young lady,' the old man sneered as he resumed his post.

"Again he spread the carmine lips of her cunt, very slowly and gradually, until it had completely disappeared. In order to get her closer to him, he was grabbing her by her buttocks.

"You would have been amazed, dear Regine, how easily that monstrous thing plunged to the lowest depths. When the old satyr began his regular and vigorous piston-like movements, far from complaining, Sally met every jab with an upward thrust of her rump.

"When he had finished, Snigger made her promise that she would not tell a soul about what had happened.

" 'If you ever mention a word and I get you in

my hands again, you will pay dearly,' he warned her. 'Now, go. I have nothing further to say to you.'

"Poor Sally knew that the threat was not a vain one. She let herself be embraced without any fuss and peacefully left.

"What do you say to that, Regine? Wouldn't you have liked to be present at a party like that?"

"I would have given anything to see something like that with my own eyes," I sighed.

"The next time something like that happens, I'll let you know, and we'll go together."

Fervently, I promised I would accompany him, and after many affectionate hugs and kisses, we separated.

CHAPTER II

MY MAID ZILLA

My father's personal entourage included a number of very polite amiable female slaves. Outwardly, their duties were domestic, but I guessed that they had other tasks. They were destined for the pleasure of the planters, whether they were married or single. But this habit did not take anything away from their respectability.

Since my father's fortune was considerable, he did things on the grandest scale. He often held dinners, whose guests were exclusively male. After the wines and liqueurs had freely circulated, overheating the brains and inflaming the imaginations, he regaled his table companions with the most suggestive lascivious dances performed by the young women mentioned above. It goes without saying that the dancers wore little or no clothing. They ended up in orgies with performers and guests rolling pell-mell on the carpet.

I had been initiated into these festivities by a nice little slave named Zilla who was a little older than I. A short time before, my father had assigned her to be my chambermaid.

It was Zilla who was always waiting when I came out of my bath, and she never seemed so delighted as when she was permitted to kiss and suck my pussy.

One time, she mentioned to me that my father had a superb prick with which he fucked with rare talent, so well, in fact, that all the girls vied for the honour of spending the night with him. She added that he never locked the door to his bedchamber, and that every night, two or three of the slaves went in because they were wild about it. Also, he adored having his prick sucked.

While telling me these things, she never stopped playing with my cunt. She stimulated it and put her fingers in. It goes without saying that they did not fail to excite me.

I asked her if she often spent the night with Papa.

"As often as the opportunity presents itself," she told me.

"But, Zilla, doesn't that cause you suffering what with such an object stuck in your belly?"

"Oh, no, not at all, Mistress. I wasn't so wide as you the first time I was fucked. Now, take your finger and see if I have a wide enough opening."

To my astonishment, three and then four of my fingers easily entered the slit.

"Oh, Zilla," I cried. "You are indeed bigger than I. But tell me, does one really have as much pleasure in fucking as one says?"

"Yes, yes!" she replied. "And how good it feels. There's nothing like it in the world. You would love it! If only you could see it done, you couldn't wait until you tried it yourself."

"Dear me!" I exclaimed. "You've aroused my curiosity. I would like to see how it is done. Couldn't you arrange to be fucked in my presence?

It goes without saying that I would be hidden and you wouldn't see me."

"Mademoiselle, I am sure that I can take care of matters so that you can have that pleasure. Nevertheless, I have to show you something beforehand. Monsieur, your father, is not home today. But we still have to be careful lest we be surprised. Come, we are going to his room."

She led me to a chamber which I had always found locked, but she had the key.

The only furniture in the room was large divans. Some lubricious pictures were hung on the walls, one of which was entirely occupied by a huge cupboard. Here and there were some large mirrors. A magnificent chandelier was suspended from the ceiling.

"There is the site where Monsieur and his friends give themselves up to their revelries, Mademoiselle. I know that Master will be here tonight."

She opened the cupboard which was filled with gauze gowns.

"We often hide here to see what is going on. Your father does not have the slightest suspicion, for he never opens this cupboard. What do you think, Mademoiselle? Why don't you hide in here this evening? You'll witness many bizarre things without anybody suspecting your presence."

"Of course I am tempted, Zilla, but what will happen if I am discovered?"

"There's little chance of that," she assured me. "But I'll disguise you in such a way that nobody will recognise you, not even under the brightest light. Just let your hand down, put on a flimsy robe like ours, and colour your arms and face with the dye I'll give you. You can remove it easily tomorrow. You'll never have a better chance. Make up your mind. I assure you that you'll be diverted. And please believe me, you won't run any risk. You'll see me fucked and many others, probably. Tell your nurse that you're going to spend the night at your father's. Come here before he leaves the dining-room and I'll hide you in the cupboard, where I won't leave you alone. I'll bring you the clothes you'll need."

I let myself be tempted, and soon, I found myself, almost naked, in the cupboard alone with a heap of gauze skirts. From time to time, Zilla, who had not abandoned me, took the chance of looking out and telling me that the coast was clear.

It was not long before my father appeared. He seemed very exhilarated. All he had on was a light dressing gown. Three girls were following him, including Zilla. Skimpy were their costumes for they consisted merely of stockings and shoes.

Papa proceeded to one of the divans which faced the cupboard. He was a little tired, he said, and asked the girls to dance and amuse themselves.

Two put their arms around each other and waltzed around the room. Their legs were tightly together. Each did her best to jut out her rump and belly.

Gradually, they became more and more animated. With sonorous slaps on their buttocks, they kept a lubricious rhythm, rubbing against each other the fleeces that adorned their mounts. Finally, as if exhausted and conquered by irresistible desires, they sank on the carpet and made *minette* to each other.

Zilla, who had not left my father's side, was cuddling his prick and caressing it with her tongue until she had rendered it to a desired state of stiffness. Giving me a malicious glance, she kept agitating it until the swollen head appeared, red and glistening like a ripe cherry.

At that moment, Papa made her turn around and whispered a few words in her ear. Then he signed to the other two girls to come and caress his gland and rump.

Zilla place one knee on each of Papa's shoulders so that her cunt was directly above his mouth. At the same moment, one of the two girls was prostrating herself between his legs which she raised and stretched, thus revealing his rear orifice into which she plunged her tongue as deep as she could.

The third took his prick in her mouth, but I observed that she carefully avoided stimulating it. She caressingly sucked the head and with her deft hands played with the little testicles.

There was a short pause.

"Just a moment, my dears," cried Papa. "Now let the hour sound."

Zilla rapidly gained the floor and hurried to ring the bell cord.

Suddenly, the door opened. Three husky Negroes, absolutely nude, erupted into the salon and set off in pursuit of the girls. Several times they succeeded in capturing them and turning them on their backs, kissing their cunts and trying to fuck them. But each time the intended victims were able to disengage themselves before the nefarious aims were carried out.

The girls disappeared, leaving alone the three men who I thought were truly comical with their big black engines, stiff as rods, jutting out before them like the prows of ships.

Discountenanced for a moment, they dashed out, one by one, in chase of the girls. One soon reappeared, dragging a girl behind him. He knocked her down on a sofa, raised her rump, and fucked her without any preliminaries. Scarcely had he begun to fuck her than a second pair made its appearance. The Negro snatched him from his task and placed his prick in the gaping cunt and began to function.

The dispossessed Negro, showing no displeasure, seized the second girl, whom he hurled on her back and promptly began to eviscerate.

The third couple showed up. The second comer had the lot of the first. He was dislodged by the newcomer who took his place.

It was like a game of musical chairs. The three men went alternatively from one to the other of the women, fucking and cramming them to the point of satiety.

Later, Zilla told me that was one of the more attractive methods of fucking.

In the midst of the general melee, the lights were suddenly extinguished. We found ourselves in complete obscurity. I heard a knock on the door of the cupboard.

"Open up, open up, Mademoiselle. Let me come in." It was Zilla.

When I opened, she rushed in, held me in her arms, and pressed me to her nude body. At the same moment, I felt a hand caressing my cunt and backside.

"Zilla, is that you who has your hands on my derriere?" I demanded.

"Oh, yes, Mademoiselle. Spread your legs. Still

more. That's just right. Lean on me and thrust out your little mount so that I can play with it."

"Oh, Zilla! But that's not your hand. Who is putting his finger in my cunt? And it's not a finger. Stop! You are hurting me! It is to help someone that you kept me in here. Whoever you are, you evil man, leave me alone. My God! He's splitting me!"

"Calm yourself, Mademoiselle. If you make any noise, we are all lost."

Then I became aware that, in spite of my resistance, a large shapely prick had plunged from behind into the depths of my vagina. Two robust arms were holding my waist and a bearded chin was resting heavily on my shoulder.

Zilla, gliding her hand between my thighs and grazing them, whispered to me in an almost inaudible voice:

"And now, dear Mademoiselle, there is no mistake about it. You are being really fucked. There's your little cunt, your brand-new cunt, being adored by a fine little bug. How does it feel? Is it good? There you are. Come now, wiggle that backside of yours. That's the best way to get full enjoyment."

Just at that moment, the door of the cupboard opened and one of the Negroes took possession of Zilla, crying: "Here she is! I've got her."

Zilla had her backside turned towards the door of the cupboard. Before she had time to emit even a squeal, the inflated spear of the black was in her aperture. It was not long before I understood from the rebounds of her body on mine that she was in the process of being superbly fucked.

The unknown behind me renewed the assault. I

was between two fires—my belly bounced against the shocks of Zilla's in front, while in the rear, my derriere received the jolts of the owner's prick which again penetrated my cunt.

Almost in a swoon, Zilla embraced me, begging: "Mistress, put your hand there and stroke John's prick which is splitting me."

I lowered my hand to the lower part of her stomach where I felt the thick and hairy lips of her cunt which were enclosing a formidable member. Both, prick and cunt, were wet with a liquid which permeated my fingers with an acrid odour that did not go away for hours.

John was not long in discharging. My friend behind was just as prompt.

Once again, darkness closed over us, and we were alone, Zilla and I.

"Zilla," I cried immediately, "take me back to my room. I am exhausted and I am frightened to death. You are a hateful strumpet, and I shall never again listen to a word you say."

"Forgive me, my dear mistress. My only wish was to see that you enjoyed yourself and to provide you with some pleasure. I'm sure that you have not been harmed or molested, so why do you hold a grudge against me? All right, I beg your pardon. An act of good will has never done anyone any harm."

I went to bed right away and fell asleep as soon as my head hit the pillow. I was exhausted.

The following morning, nevertheless, rested and refreshed from my bath, I was in a better humour and joked with my maid about the events of the previous evening. But I could not get out of her the identity of my assailant who had had me in the cupboard in dog fashion. But I had an idea that I could not shake out of my head.

Well, I had been fucked twice, but, to tell the truth, in the ordinary fashion. Therefore, I wanted to see Dick as soon as possible to give me a lesson which would satisfy me better. I did not have to wait long. With a radiant face, Dick arrived that very afternoon.

He informed me that a girl who had proved to be too lazy, along with two others, was to be handed over to Snigger at four that afternoon. He had been able to get a key to the barn which was to be the site of correction. The granary was half filled with dried flax. By displacing several crates and thanks to several large cracks in the floor of the loft where we had concealed ourselves, we were assured of the best seats in the house; we would not miss a detail of what would happen below us.

"Hurry up, Regine!" he commanded. "Get your clothes on. We have just the time to take our places before the play begins."

We ran there furiously. Once in the loft, Dick carefully locked the door.

We made ourselves a comfortable niche in the flax just above a large hole in the floor.

"From this location," Dick declared, "we shall have a general view of the operations which that bastard Snigger is going to commit on the behinds and cunts of the poor girls."

Once our accommodations were completed, Dick lifted up my skirts and lowered his pants. We lay in a position so that he could easily see and explore the secret valley hidden between my thighs, and, in turn, I could inspect the mysterious charms of his dear little pipe with the sacks dangling from it.

While we were doing that, I recounted to him the spectacle I had witnessed the previous night, but I believed it would be discreet not to mention the part I was forced to take in it. In turn, he mentioned he had seen his father have intercourse with young slave girls. He said that one evening, he heard a racket. Noiselessly, he got up and silently made his way to the doorway of the salon. Through a chink in the door, he had seen his father, armed with a supple birch switch, chasing around the room four nude Negresses and switching them on the buttocks.

"He finally caught one, whom he spread on a table with her buttocks raised and her legs wide apart. The three others came to his rescue by opening the flabby lips of the victim's cunt and introducing my father's member into it. While he was fucking, they tickled his balls and prick.

"You can well imagine the interest with which I followed this game," Dick continued. "Inadvertently, I leaned too hard on the door and it opened. Imagine the surprise of the participants. One of the women grabbed hold of me and dragged me into the centre of the salon.

"My father made me take off my nightshirt, and to punish me for my espionage instead of being in bed where I belonged, he decided that I was going to get a good spanking. One of the women was ready to carry out the order, when another, whose clitoris I had often tickled, clutched my prick, came up with the idea that one of them would lie under me while the others would fustigate me.

"The proposition was enthusiastically accepted. She who had proposed the punishment was invited to take the indicated position. (The sly girl probably had that in mind all along.)

"Consequently, she stretched out on one of the mats on the parquet and placed me on top of her. Dare I confess, dear Regine, that I made not the slightest resistance? I quickly adopted the most favourable position to taste her charms to the full. But I did not count on the other three who inflicted on me an agonising torture.

"They took hold of my prick, the head of which they passed around the lips of the avaricious. It was in vain for me to try and force myself upward with the hope of penetrating. Just at the moment I was about to succeed, the enraged females dragged me off, rendering my efforts in vain. At that, they laughed so hard that they had to hold their sides. My father, too, was howling with laughter at my predicament.

"I implored them to let me finish with my girl, although I was raging inside.

" 'Oh, let him go ahead,' interrupted my partner. 'Can't you see that I am also dying for it?'

"They were moved. My executioners decided to place me in the right position, and, with a single shove, my javelin darted into the gaping redoubt. What a delicious warmth I found there. And how my hussy knew how to respond to each thrust.

"Increasingly aroused, she finished by imprisoning me tightly between her legs, while her companions, with their birch switches, gently beat me on my buttocks.

" 'Strike! Strike!' I yelled. 'If you wish, you can flay me. Hit harder. Harder, I say.'

"All my sensations seemed to be concentrated in

my prick. I thought I was being lowered into a bath of bliss.

"The enthusiastic women unanimously declared that I fucked like a man and that, henceforth, I was worthy to join the ranks of fuckers.

"Oh, my beloved Regine. You have procured for me an equal pleasure. With your wonderful sucking as you cuddled my testicles and excited my behind, you have sent me to paradise. Did you swallow my seed, dearest?"

"Yes, indeed, Dick. I didn't lose a drop."

"That's good, Regine. In exchange, I am going to attempt to give you the same pleasure. Let me put this bale of flax under your adorable behind to raise it up. Now put one of your hands on each side. That's perfect. Legs apart now so that I can titillate your little hole with my tongue."

Then, reclining on the bench, Dick ardently licked the hole of my derriere. He jabbed in his tongue as well as he could, and he was so successful that I felt it wiggle inside of me, arousing unusual sensations in all my amorous portions.

Until that moment, I had never realised all the joys that were contained in our derrieres or the close connection of them with our cunts. There was a silence of a few moments.

"Do you like it when someone does the rose leaf to you?" Dick asked me. "That is the name for what I just did to you."

"Ah, how good it was, my dear Dick!" I exclaimed. "It was the sweetest experience I have ever undergone."

"Does that enhance the pleasure your cunt felt?"

"Yes, but in such a strange way."

"Did you feel as if you were about to get wet?" he inquired.

"More than that!" I exclaimed. "It seemed as if my backside and cunt were on fire. One more little suck, my dear Dick, and a little dig with the thing and then it will come."

"At your service, Mademoiselle. Now place your hands as they were before. Spread open the lips of your little dear love hole. Show me the most sensitive spot and tell me what can best excite it."

I put my hands under my thighs and, opening the labia, I gently ran the tip of my finger on my clitoris and between the little lips of my vagina.

"There it is, Dick. That's the most tender spot."

"Well, Regine, I'll lick the entrance while you agitate the button. Tell me what you feel, and, above all, tell me when you are about to reach your climax."

"Oh, Dick, my pussy is getting as hot as a furnace the more you suck me and I stroke myself. Oh, how marvellous that feels! I can't remain still. The cheeks of my backside are twitching. I have to lift myself up. Oh, Dick. Suck! Suck! Suck my little cunt as hard as you can. Push your tongue in as far as it will go. Ah, that's it. Squeeze my behind cheeks tightly together. Stick your finger in there. Oh, my darling. Oh, Dick. It is coming. My God, the pleasure is ineffable!"

I fell in a faint while Dick savoured the sweet liquid which was escaping from my source of delights.

Just at that moment . . . But since that deserves another chapter, we shall stop here.

CHAPTER III

LIZZY

We were interrupted in the midst of our delicious transports by steps which were mounting the stairs leading to the loft. Dick just had enough time to throw on us several armsful of flax when the door opened. To my great fright, I heard the voice of my father ring in my ears.

He was accompanied by a young woman whom I had never seen before. Later, I learned that her name was Lizzy. Tenderly, he arranged for her a comfortable seat not two steps from our hiding place.

"Here we are, Lizzy, my darling, free from all prying eyes. From here we can amuse ourselves by watching Snigger and his girls. It has come to my ears that he has two young girls whom he is going to fuck, either before or after the chastisement. But, my dear, why don't you take off some of your clothes? It is terribly hot in this loft, and you can always put your corset back on when we go back."

"Are you sure, Robert, that no one can see us here?" she asked worriedly.

"How could that be possible? We found the door locked, and I carefully closed and latched it once we were inside."

He removed his jacket so that he could lie down.

She, in turn, took off all her garments except her shift and let down her hair. Through the wisps of flax I could make out that she was young, charming, and had a flawless complexion. Dick whispered to me that she was the wife of a neighbouring planter named Hobbs who was a notorious debauchee. While he claimed a ferocious jealousy for his wife, he shamelessly deceived her with innumerable mistresses of every hue.

"It was good of you, Lizzy, to have come today as soon as you knew of my feelings for you. How were you able to escape the ogre?" asked my father, referring to her husband.

"I pretended I had to do some shopping in the village, and, to make him feel good, I promised to inquire about some cigars he had ordered and had not yet received. As you see, instead of going to town, I have come here."

Papa warmly embraced her.

"Take it out yourself, my treasure. It adores your fingers which are so agile and gentle. When it feels them, it is given a new life."

She did not lose her calm when she unbuttoned the trousers, opened the fly, slid her hand inside where she fumbled around, and finally brought to light an inviting prick.

It was my father's gland. By instinct and good-breeding, I should have turned away my eyes. But I have to tell the truth. I was so excited that I could not help but regarding it with the deepest interest. Above all, I was struck by the whiteness of the skin and the haughty mien the head presented when Lizzy brought it forth. She fondled the infuriated organ and brought it to her mouth.

"Tell me its name, Lizzy," my father asked her.

"Prick," she simply replied, raising her eyes to it.

"And that adorable little hole with its fine silky moustaches, what do you call that, my dear?"

"Cunt," she answered with a lascivious smile.

"Perfect. And now, what are we going to do with this prick and this delicious cunt?"

"Unite them," she said, "to prove that they have been made for no other purpose than fucking."

"Does the ogre fuck you often, my dear friend?"

"Just now and then. But sometimes he gets the fantasy to introduce his dirty piece into my rear, and I suffer horribly."

"He's a brute. But, on the other hand, my love, to bugger or be buggered is a wonderful thing when it is skilfully done."

"Oh, Robert, do what you want with me. Fuck me any way you have a mind to."

"Thank you, darling. Well, let's see how things go. The beast never fucked you before any one of your slaves, did he?"

"Oh, yes," Lizzy cried. "More than once, he forced me to be present at his foul orgies. I had to suck his gland just after he had pulled it out of some cunt. One time, when I refused to commit such a degrading action, he summoned one of the Negro men who stripped me to the buff, spread my legs apart, and fucked and fucked me while I was standing. Everybody was watching."

"What a scoundrel he must be! How I loathe him. I would give anything to snatch you away from him. Nevertheless, looking at it from all sides, it is better that you remain with him and come and see me as often as possible. Oh, look! Here's the first girl, a cheeky little slut. I have ordered that she be given a dozen, and I trust the old goat will not spare her. Get on your knees, my dear, and while you are looking through the crack in the plank, I'll try the little rear crack we were talking about a minute ago."

Snigger took the note that was handed to him. After reading it, he made a face as if he were trying to smile. Then he patted the hands of the trembling young girl.

"Oh, my dear Mr Snigger," she snivelled. "This is the first time I have been sent here. Won't you be so good as not to undress me?"

"Well, we'll have to see about that," answered the old sadist. "Whatever we do, you have to take your place here."

As was his custom, he positioned her on the bench, her belly resting on it and her breasts dangling down. When he tried to lift her skirt, she began to scream to the high heavens and kick like a mule.

"Ha! Ha!" he snickered. "Everything is just fine now. I'm just putting things in order."

Taking hold of a long piece of rope, he tied each leg to the ends of the bench and spread them as wide as possible. He paid no attention to her piercing bawls, but calmly and libidinously ran his lewd hands over her stomach and buttocks. Then he slipped them under her thighs and, extending the lips of her slit, he inserted his finger in the abyss.

She spouted the most vile invectives at him, but her abuse seemed to have no result but to enhance the enjoyment he was having. Laughing heartily, he produced his venerable tool, placed the gleaming head between the lips abundantly adorned with hair, and slowly plunged it into the opening.

"What in the world is he doing?" I heard my father say to Madame Hobbs.

"He's admiring her ebony opulent rear, and he's ogling the other hair below. That's where he's inserting his prick. Good. He's got it into the hilt. Now he's got her by the haunches. Go to it! Go to it! He's shoving. He's shoving. He's stuffing her. Now he's fucking her with all his might."

"Well, darling, I think we should have our own little party, don't you agree? Wouldn't your dear little cunt like to feel in its mouth the taste of my little dick?"

"Oh, it is just dying for it. Your adorable member fills it with delight and felicity. How wonderful it is to be fucked by a man who you love. Does my poor little aperture embrace amorously enough its valiant chevalier?"

"Darling, your delicious lips hug it so delightfully that I am out of my mind. Give me your hands so that your satiny fingers can cuddle my balls."

In the meanwhile, Snigger, having had his full of his victim, withdrew his piston and dried it.

"And now, Mademoiselle," he said with a leer, "we are going to settle accounts for all the vile insults you showered on me. What do you think about that? Swish! And this! Smack!"

The cat-o'-nine-tails flayed pitilessly the buttocks, the haunches, and every part of the girl's body.

"Oh, have pity on me, Mr Snigger. I'll never say bad things to you ever again," she wailed.

"Really?" The vicious whip fell again on her body.

"I'll let you fuck me as much as you want."

"Thank you very much. That's very generous of you. Now you want me to fuck you," he said sarcastically.

By now, she had received a good dozen solid blows. The old man stepped back to survey his work. The poor girl's buttocks were furrowed with wide red streaks.

"Dear Mr Snigger, I beseech you! Have pity on my poor behind. Have mercy and let me go."

"Oh! Oh! We're not quits yet. And besides, my beauty, don't you want me to fuck you again? Perhaps you wouldn't like that."

"Yes! But my derriere is on fire and I feel that my cunt is ablaze. Go ahead. Fuck! I couldn't wish for anything better than that right now."

The old lecher! Lasciviously, he dampened two of his fingers in the moist cunt and introduced them into the rear orifice. The poor thing gave a start.

"Do you want to feel that cat again?" he inquired with an evil grin.

"Not that, Mr Snigger, not for anything in the world. I'd just like to feel your great big handsome prick, there . . . inside my cunt."

"Well, that's reasonable. Now, get on your back."

To the best of her capacity, she extended her front while the lecher removed his trousers and shirt, stroked his gland two or three times, and then inserted the organ into the aperture.

"Does it feel good?" he groaned.

"Oh, it's exquisite, Mr Snigger!"

She gave a little squeal as the prick began to impale her. With a powerful lurch and a clutch at her sides, he plunged the organ into her very entrails. Then he withdrew it, except the head, thrusting it in again, pulling it out, jabbing it in, continuing until he had reached the paroxysm of bliss and discharged.

"Lizzy, what's he doing?" Papa asked.

"My word! The dotard is now in her again and the girl doesn't seem to mind too much."

"Maybe she has a taste for it. Suppose I did the same to you, Lizzy, what would you say?"

"You have my permission, Robert. Go ahead. I can't refuse you anything. But please go easy."

"Have no fears about that, my dear. Open it as well as you can. Now. Do you feel it? It's starting to go in. It has entered. Am I hurting you?"

"Oh no, my dear. You are not making me suffer at all. It is a wonderful sensation. Go ahead. Shove harder. See if you can't get farther in. Your prick, no matter where it may go, will never wound me."

Papa held her firmly, leaned over on her back, and put his hands on her cunt. I saw Madame Hobbs twitch with pleasure as the prick slowly began to go into operation. This scene drove Dick nearly mad with excitement. He could not help but pat my backside. I knew what he wanted and I told him, "Go ahead."

I confess that the view of the coming and going of Papa's prick between Lizzy's two superb globes aroused in me all my innate lasciviousness and I was crying for a prick.

"I'm going to dip it a little into your pussy," Dick declared. "Put your hands behind you and spread your legs."

I did as he said, and immediately I felt his gland on the spot.

"Oh, it's almost juicy. Stimulate my cunt a little more. Oh, how good that feels . . . "

"It feels as good to me."

The pleasure became so intense that we could not contain ourselves much longer. In spite of ourselves, we had to cry out: "How wonderful it is!"

"What's that?" exclaimed my father. "My God! It's Dick fucking with Regine like a madman. Ah, that scamp Dick! Good manners demand that you come to me first for permission to fuck my daughter so freely. Well, I have the feeling that you acquitted yourself well and I forgive you."

I did not have the slightest doubt that my father, on discovering us, was more pleased than angry. Something untoward could happen, however, and it was convenient to have under his thumb good Dick to whom the responsibility could be imputed. Consequently, when I made my way out from under the flax, he lifted me in his arms, planted a kiss on each of my cheeks, and told me not to worry, for he was not irritated with me. Then he lifted my skirts so that Madame Hobbs could see all of my pussy.

"What do you think, Lizzy. Doesn't she have an adorable little boutique? So chubby. The skin is so satiny and the red is so delightful."

Regarding it, Madame Hobbs put her lips to it, a movement which made her raise her backside. Throwing a glance at Dick, he pointed it out with his finger.

"My dear Lizzy," he cried, "our friend Dick is admiring and devouring with his eyes your superb posterior attractions. There is no doubt he is dying

41

to make a closer inspection, but I wager that Regine has drained him dry for the moment."

Dick contented himself with an ironic smile, and placed his hands on Madame's behind.

"Do you mind, Madame?"

"Indeed no. Since you saw everything that went on here, I would be impolite if I said no. As long as you promise to be discreet and never breathe a word to a soul, I know of no reason why you should not share in our romps."

Dick relished the thought of soon making the acquaintance of a new altar of love. Pressing her tightly against him, he slapped her bottom and his fingers explored every recess of her slit, first separating the moist lips fringed with blonde fleece.

"Your pussy could not be more seductive than it is now," said Dick. "Its silken tresses are adorable!"

He put his words into action by sweeping his member back and forth through the beauties he had just lauded. Madame Hobbs began to laugh. Very proud of the praise bestowed on her by the young man, she spread her legs and elevated her perfectly contoured derriere.

Madame Hobbs buttressed herself on her hands and knees and Dick started having her in the manner of dogs.

A racket now resounded in the room below, a din which naturally attracted our attention. We hurried to the openings and saw that the spectacle had changed.

The wretched victim of the sadistic Snigger had disappeared to be replaced by two newcomers. They were husky young girls, and the lecher was hard put to defend himself against their attack.

One had grabbed him in her robust arms while

the other tied his hands with cord. When they had fettered him, they dragged him by the end of a rope to a pulley suspended from the ceiling. Then they fastened one end of the rope to the bonds tying the hands of the flogger. When this was done, they pulled on the other end with the result that poor Mr Snigger was dangling in the air.

He was cursing and mouthing oaths like mad. But the two girls were splitting their sides with laughter as they told him that finally his turn had come. They added that he was going to get what was richly due him including the feel of the cat-o'-nine-tails. One mentioned almost casually that she was going to see that his rancid prick would be put into such a state that it would be useless for at least a month.

Pulling down his pants and raising his shirt, the one went behind to whip his behind unmercilessly while the other, in front, stroked his prick. Flagellated in the rear and masturbated in the front, he was not slow in discharging. At first, he did not seem too displeased. But when he saw them return from a second, and then a third, engagement, he began to complain bitterly and his poor member was reduced to nothing.

"It's useless to keep on," remarked the one. "His prick is as limp as a wet rag."

"Show him your cunt up close," advised the other as she contined swishing the wicked whip.

Her companion lifted her skirt, and, spreading wide apart the thick lips of her generous cunt, she placed it directly before his eyes, allowing him to see all the way down to the depths of the fiery cavern. Snigger, the poor devil, probably for the first time in his life, turned away his view from this enchanting tableau and wearily closed his eyes.

"Bring him back to life!" angrily cried the flogger. "There is nothing equal to what John told me about."

The girl who had been in charge of the victim's virility took a table, pushed it near the patient, climbed on top of it, and stuck her odoriferous opening right before his nose. Her companion, passing her hands between the legs of the lost soul, shook his moribund member and sagging testicles with such vigour that in a few moments, they made him discharge a fourth time.

Thoroughly worn out, the wretch seemed on the point of fainting. At that point, the two executioners decided to cut him down, and while he was lying almost lifeless on the floor, they declared in solemn tones:

"Remember, if you dare say a word about us, we'll not be slow in telling everybody about the brilliant exploits that we have just made you accomplish. Would you like to be the laughing-stock of the whole plantation?"

Thereupon they left, congratulating each other on their success and making a mock reverence to him.

We could not help but laugh at the risible scene. And we agreed with Madame Hobbs who was of the opinion that he only got what was coming to him.

CHAPTER IV

I LEAVE HOME

In hot countries, frequent baths are not a luxury but a necessity. My father fully realised that, and since he was very fastidious about his person and meticulous in matters of hygiene, he communicated his habits to his entourage. And he provided facilities in the form of numerous showers throughout his plantation.

I had my baths as regularly as I had my meals. Because of the stifling, humid heat, I had two baths every day, and often three.

For me, the height of pleasure was to have Zilla in the tub with me. She was always witty and amusing. Before putting back on our clothes, we had the habit of stretching out on a bed, where we delighted in the absolute freedom of our bodies, happy to be free from the complication of hooks and snaps and corsets, which are the base of the feminine toilette.

The sight and scent of our nudity then led us naturally to intimate conversations, mostly of a passionate nature. Zilla, in particular, liked to lead the way to such lubricious topics. She made motions and said things to arouse my baser desires. Sometimes she persuaded me to describe the sensations I felt in the course of my libertine larks and to tell her my delight in breathing and manipulating the instruments of love. Other times, she had the whim to kiss me and play with my pussy and put me in various positions. In other words, we gave ourselves up to all sorts of extravagances and follies.

Later I learned that the purpose of these divertissements was to provide amusement to my father who was able to witness and hear all our girlish pranks through a peek-hole.

In the course of one of our frolics, I asked Zilla to tell me which gave her the most pleasure, a black or a white prick.

She replied that in such matters, colour was of little matter. From her own experience, she could state that from the point of view of vigour and activity, the one was equal to the other. But she finally admitted that for herself, she preferred to be fucked by a white, because certain blacks, particularly John were endowed with unbelievably enormous members.

"My dear little mistress," she added, "when you first see one of them, you would not believe your eyes. You are sure that one would rip you wide open. But once it manages to get inside of you, your only thought is to extract all enjoyment possible from the monstrous engine."

"I certainly would like to undergo a sensation like that!" I exclaimed. "Do you think you could get one for me?"

"Well, Mademoiselle Regine, why don't you take my place tonight. I assure you that you will be served as perfectly as you could wish. As a matter of fact, I have promised John to spend an hour with him. In the darkness, he would not recognise the difference between you and me."

Consequently, we agreed to change beds that night. I begged her to tell me a little about the manner of operation of my future fucker. Here is what she told me:

"As you can imagine, he expects that the door will be easily opened. Also, he promised me to come in silently without saying a word. As soon as he will have found the bed, you can be sure that his hands will be under the sheets and he will be investigating your behind and cunt. More than likely, he will drag you to the edge of the bed, place your legs on each of his shoulders, and suck your clitoris. If you want to be nice to him and give him some pleasure, you will stretch out your hand and seize his mighty organ. Play with it gently, and when you feel that it is hard, bring it to your mouth. Then let things take their course."

That evening, Zilla smeared my slit with certain herbs which had a subtle and penetrating aroma. John, she said, adored strong perfumes. My maid made the bed meticulously. It was in a spacious room with a verandah not far from mine. As soon as night fell, I took her place. It was only a few minutes before I heard the door softly open and somebody crossing across the room. The person seemed to know his way.

Now near my bed, the visitor lifted the covers and I felt a big clammy hand lift up my nightgown and touch my Venus mount. The other hand slipped under my buttocks, and I was slowly pulled to the edge of the bed, with my legs dangling down. A fuzzy head popped up between my thighs, and a nose noisily inhaled all around my crevice while a dancing tongue ran over all the region around my cunt. When John realised from my jerks and sighs that voluptuousness was being born in me, he began to suck more ardently. Taking hold of the hemispheres of my derriere, he slapped them so soundly with his ham-like hand that it hurt and I could barely restrain a cry of pain.

Nevertheless, it was not long before the burning on my derriere was augmenting considerably the sensuousness of all my pussy. Clutching his head, I held it fast between my spread legs. Then, drawing back, I pressed my fiery clitoris with all my force on the intoxicating tongue, so successfully that the moment came, intense, and I felt myself inundated with a hot and sticky liquid.

"Miss Zilla," he suddenly asked in an astonished tone. "You have such a tiny cunt. And what happened to your beautiful hair? I can't even get a hold on you."

Only then did an idea come to me. Zilla and I had about the same figure and complexion, but there was one big difference between us. Her mound was adorned with a thick bush of hair while mine had scarcely a hair of the luxurious thicket that now covers it.

"Oh, that's too bad," continued John. "I suppose you must have shaved it off. But it did smell so good."

Nevertheless, he continued to kiss my hairless pussy with enthusiasm, all the while licking it with his thick tongue. He then begged me to put my hand on his monster.

When I hesitated, he put it there himself. My God in Heaven! What a prick! I do not exaggerate when I say that it was at least a foot in length and as thick in proportion. But its head was unbelievable. I am not lying when I say that it was as big as my clenched fist. Contemplating the prodigy with despondency, I seriously began to worry about my poor little cunt.

"Ha, ha! What do you think now, Miss? Do you think it can go in? You're trembling like a leaf. John's toy is big, I admit, but it is as agile as a serpent. It goes into a cunt like a thread into a needle. We'll soon see. But first you have to give it a kiss with your mouth. That stimulates it."

He pushed toward my mouth that fat column. Holding it in both my hands, I felt that it was robust and throbbing with life. Although I was positive that my mouth would never contain it, I inserted it between my lips. But, miracle of miracles, my mouth took it in its entirety. My poor mouth was stuffed and my cheeks were inflated from the pressure. Never, never before had I had such a mouthful.

"Oh, Miss. That's wonderful. You're magnificent!" he groaned as he forced his member deeper into my mouth.

I had already tasted on several occasions Dick's sperm, now I had the fantasy to compare his with John's. I sucked John's enormous gland the best I could while manipulating his distended testicles which were as heavy as sacks of gold.

The prick expanded still more and became harder and hotter. Suddenly, a wave of boiling sperm shot forth in my mouth, so abruptly and with such force that I could not swallow it all. Some of it dribbled from the corners of my mouth. I found it thick and aromatically tasty.

Beside himself with voluptuousness, all John could do was moan: "Oh, that was famous," and then with an expiring sigh, he rolled over on his side.

While this was going on, there was a big ruckus on the other side of the bed. I heard the muffled laughs of Zilla from which I concluded that she and my father were not wasting their time and were having their own little love duet. Contenting myself with drying my mouth, I awaited what was to come next.

John quickly came to. He placed his hands under my buttocks and recommenced his *minette* on me. Then, straightening up, he drew me to the edge of the bed and placed himself between my legs which he put on his shoulders. Now we were at the point I both dreaded and ardently desired.

"Ha, ha! What are you thinking of, Miss? Do you think it will go in? Don't shake so much."

I felt the redoubtable organ pushing its round head against my cunt. At the vigorous attack, the delicate aperture seemed to dilate beyond belief. But I had made up my mind to endure every conceivable measure in order that the operation would be a success. With my fingers, I expanded my labia as far as they would go. With a formidable thrust, John was able to get the head only halfway down. Opening my thighs still wider, I shoved up my derriere to meet his plunge, but, in spite of all efforts, the prick remained where it was, unable to descend any farther.

Suddenly, the Negro seemed struck with an idea. Withdrawing his instrument, he began to soak his virility and my nook with an abundance of spittle. After this, he resumed his position and renewed his efforts. This time, things went better. The mighty head, now well lubricated, gradually forced its way, and, finally, I had the supreme joy of feeling this majestic specimen of virility penetrating in its entirety into my being.

I was beside myself, releasing a scream of triumph and relief.

"At last I have it! It's inside! I feel it all in me!"

Zilla, with a peal of laughter, cried: "Hold on to it, my dear mistress. Don't let it go. And you, John, don't hold yourself back. Give her a good fuck!"

"So it's you, Zilla. You . . . ! So you make fun of John today. Tomorrow John will make fun of you."

"Go ahead and fuck her, you damned fool!" cried Zilla, and hurling herself behind him, she stuck her hand between us, touching my labia which enclosed tightly John's magnificent prick.

"Fuck, you idiot. You should get down on your knees and thank your lucky star for having obtained the most admirable cunt in all the islands."

The Negro finally understood.

"Oh, Miss Regine, you are too kind to poor John. You have such a pretty little cunt, and I am going to make you happy."

He began a series of motions, each more delicious than the other. Lasciviously, he grazed his imperious sceptre across the moist lips of my blazing orifice. I though I was on the verge of death.

Zilla's fingers which were titillating my clitoris and my father's balls which were tickling my posterior opening enhanced my raptures.

We had tried everything and I am sure that the good Lord had granted all our desires. But our good fortune was not at an end. The best was to come.

In my cunt, I had the biggest and most splendid prick that I had ever seen. The agile fingers of Zilla were stimulating my clitoris. And I still was not satisfied.

Suddenly, Zilla, as if she had arrived at the paroxysm of erotic folly, redoubled her caresses and then, prey to a veritable venereal delirium, screamed in a quavering voice:

"Forward! Be bold! Onward. Fuck! Fuck! Fuck! Pricks, fuck! Cunts, suck! Balls, ejaculate! . . . Forward. Shoot, shoot in every direction! Fuck! Fuck! Fuck!"

She continued that way, wildly, fumingly, out of her mind, until the moment when a torrent of sperm simultaneously gushed from the pricks, the backsides, the cunts, the testicles, bestowing on us a joy without name, which caused us to roll pell-mell on each other, knocking us unconscious with voluptuousness.

We finally recovered our senses. Odd is the only adjective that can be employed to describe our formation.

John had in his mouth my father's prick, but his big white bewildered eyes, rolling in their orbits, seemed to be searching for something else to suck. Papa appeared to be wild with desire. Zilla had arranged herself so that her source of delight was glued to my mouth. Distractedly, I made *minette* to her, nibbling her clitoris, which caused her to drench my face with a copious emission.

Several moments passed. Finally, we agreed that we had quaffed sufficiently from the cup of love and separated to go to our own beds for much needed repose to restore our exhausted energies.

From that day on, my father showed himself to be more tender and affectionate than ever to me.

After a certain period of time, he made up his

mind to send me to the southern part of the United States to attend a girls' school there. He told me that one of his friends, Captain St Jean, would take charge of me and bring me to New Orleans on his schooner. The ship would lift anchor in two weeks, he added.

I thanked him and approved of his decision and promised to be ready by the time of departure. To be sure, it grieved me to separate myself from him, but now that I knew him better, I could appreciate his decision. Also, the thought of widening my horizons and making new friends made my chagrin easier to bear.

I was not the only one about to leave the plantation. Dick, also, was to leave. His father was sending him to study medicine at a university on one of the islands. My beloved and I promised to exchange letters regularly. He vowed to remain faithful to me, but he burst out laughing when I demanded that he send me a detailed description of all the girls he fell in love with and of the sexual games he had with them. I realised, of course, that he could not lead a celibate life at his age.

"Remember," I enjoined him, "I don't care how many girls you have. I'll forgive you as long as you have confidence in me and you tell me faithfully everything that happens."

I have to say that Dick faithfully kept his word by sending me numerous accounts of his amorous encounters. I have kept them all, and they are so amusing and delightful that perhaps, one day, I shall have them printed for the diversion of my readers.

BOOK II

CHAPTER V

THE VOYAGE

My preparations for the trip were finished. My father brought me aboard the trim schooner, the *Carmarilla*, and turned me over to his friend, Captain Saint-Jean.

My chambermaid Zilla was to be my companion on the voyage. She was most enthusiastic, not only at the prospect of a new existence but by my father's promise to emancipate her if she served me faithfully until I was twenty-one.

When I was on board, I was happy to find a charming and very pretty young girl, whom the captain presented to me as his niece Laura.

Since the ship was to lift anchor the first thing the next morning, we immediately began to make ourselves as comfortable as possible. There was placed at my disposition a stateroom, tiny but very elegantly decorated. It was adjoining Laura's. On the other side of the salon were two similar cabins occupied respectively by the Captain and by the first mate, Mr William Yeats, a very distinguished young man who showered us with his attentions.

Zilla had been installed in a comfortable stateroom near the prow of the ship where the junior officers had their quarters. They were enchanted with her for she was an outrageous flirt.

Captain Saint-Jean was a plump man apt to lose his temper but possessing a good heart. Although he was a widower and fifty years old, he was still young in heart. He adored the weaker sex, and it did not take me long to guess in which direction his admiration was aimed.

Laura waited on me hand and foot and revealed herself to be very communicative. Because the Captain and the first mate were preoccupied with the preparations for the departure, we were left to ourselves more or less the first evening on board. Laura showed me how to arrange my things "ship-shape," that is to say, to make the best use of the limited space available to us.

She told me that it was the first voyage that she was making with her uncle, who was also her guardian. Not having any permanent home, she preferred by far to be at sea with her captain than to remain alone on shore. She added that the Captain had at times quite curious habits. Without the slightest thought, he took the greatest liberties with women who did not put up too much of a resistance.

"But, after all, Regine, how monotonous life would be if we were always stiff and formal, and if we did not accept at times some pleasantries in good humour," she concluded. "And they certainly are not dangerous."

I replied that I was entirely of her mind and that, although I was still young in years, I had seen enough of life to recognise the truth of the proverb, "Every woman has in her heart a dormant whore." Candidly, I said that I did not know the full significance of it.

Bursting out into peals of laughter, Laura

declared herself ready to complete my education if I was agreeable.

"Nevertheless," she observed, "I am sure that you have been at a good school and that there is not much more to teach you."

Towards evening, the Captain and the mate came down to the salon where they concocted some grog, which they asked us to share with them.

After we had sipped the steaming hot beverage, the Captain advised us to get to bed early because we would be awakened very early in the morning by the racket caused by the departure.

As he wished me good night, he called me his dear child and said that he loved me, not only because of my father who was his best friend, but because of myself, my goodness, and my innocence. With that, he drew me to him, kissed me on both cheeks, and ordered his niece to see that I would be comfortable in my cabin.

The next day before dawn, the bustle on the decks and the creaking of the ropes broke my slumber. It was not long before I felt the ship pitch and heave, which meant the wind was in the sails and we were on the high seas.

At first, the rolling was not unpleasant, but soon I began to recognise that it was having a disastrous effect on my internal organs. For the first time in my life, I was experiencing the horrors of seasickness. The more the ship pitched and rolled, the more my agony increased. I hurled my self on my bunk, moaning, and remained there.

After a period which seemed interminable, the stewardess came and asked what I would like for lunch. I told her that I did not want a thing, but I asked her to send Zilla to me for I was not at all well. She informed me that Zilla was in the same state as I, and Laura, too, but that she was going to report to the Captain.

The hearty tar almost immediately was knocking at my door. I asked him to enter. He approached my pillow, regarded me with a tender look, advised me to take some nourishment, and tried to comfort me by saying that I would be feeling better soon.

"Oh!" I weakly replied. "The mere thought of food is nauseating. I am sure that I am going to die shortly."

"Nonsense," he laughed as he held up my head slightly. "You're not that far gone yet. Look, you're alive and breathing."

He had his arms around my bust, and, sick as I was, I noticed how his eyes glittered at the sight of my breasts visible through the diaphanous material of my nightgown.

"Oh, put me back down. I feel so terrible," I groaned.

He lay my head back down on the pillows, and while arranging my night dress, he ran his hand over my breast.

"Why, you seem to have a bit of a fever," he exclaimed as if he were surprised. "Don't you think I should take off some of these heavy blankets?"

With a nod of my head, I acquiesced. Then he stroked the upper part of my thighs, stopping at my stomach.

"Is that where it hurts?" he asked.

"Oh, yes, Captain. I'm so sick."

"Yes, I can see that you are not feeling well, my poor child. But I know something that will do you good. A hot spiced rum. I'll make one for you."

"Please don't bother. I wouldn't have the strength to drink it."

But he paid me no attention. He went out and soon returned with the boiling beverage. After cajoling me, I tried it and, to my surprise, I was able to get a good part of it down. Afterwards, I was overcome by a sort of torpor, but my sensation of nausea was somewhat allayed. I lay there, absolutely without any strength or will. It was as if my brain were an absolute vacuum.

The Captain then began to arrange my berth. Meeting with no resistance, he slipped his hands under my shift between my thighs until he came to my *mons veneris*. Pursing his lips, he gingerly inserted a finger in the narrow slit. Then he lifted my nightgown up to my waist and passionately kissed my pussy.

"What are you doing there?" I feebly demanded.

"I'm just looking after my poor sick little girl," he answered as he kissed me on the forehead and went out.

For the entire day, I was literally inert. The seasickness had weakened me, and the alcohol had so dazed me that I was incapable of the slightest movement. I was indifferent to everything around me. All I remember is that the Captain came several times to see how I was. And I am quite sure that he took advantage of my condition to take all possible liberties, not denying himself the privilege of contemplating and caressing my secret beauties.

At twilight, Laura came to visit me, bringing some tea which I found stimulating and refreshing. She told me that she, too, had been violently ill. It was because of the weather which was unusually rough and the schooner had to fight against an unfavourable wind. She wanted to know if the Captain had been to see me and if he had taken care of me.

I told her that he had come several times and that he made me drink a rum that practically made me unconscious. And I said that I was positive that he had done to me what no honourable man would have done to a helpless girl.

"I understand," Laura replied with a grin. "That's his usual approach, and I know from experience what is coming next. I know the old salt too well. Why should I conceal it from you? I am something more than a niece to my uncle, and that is how he began with me. I am positive that he wants to commence intimate relations with you. Oh, don't worry. I'm not jealous in the least. He will not limit himself to the liberties he had already taken as long as you are unable to defend yourself. But, tell me, are you really afraid of his advances?"

As she was saying this, her hand was descending down my thighs.

"Oh, Regine!" she exclaimed. "What a delicious little snare you have. I'm not surprised that the Captain returned so often to look at it after having made such a delightful discovery. But it is so wide. Now don't try to fool me, you gay deceiver. You're not as innocent as you like to let on. Oh, you are going to have to tell me all your adventures. In turn, I'll tell you mine, and that will create an intimacy between us. Until that time comes, my dear friend, put your hand there and stroke me a little while we kiss to seal our pact."

Sitting on the edge of my berth, she lifted her skirts, took my hand and guided it through her hot, firm thighs to a thick bouquet of silky hair which adorned their junction. At that spot, I felt the development of two adorable chubby lips. To content her, I slid my fingers in the moist crevice.

"Hee, hee! You're not so tight, either, Laura," I declared as I inserted two fingers into the opening.

"And why should I be?" she retorted with a saucy look. "It should be big enough to receive visitors. Didn't you know that?"

"Indeed, I did not. What do you mean by saying it should be able to receive guests?" I asked in turn, trying to look as ingenuous as possible.

"Don't try to make fun of me," she admonished. "You know as well as I what sort of visitors we like to introduce in these salons. I'll bet you anything that you know the name of those guests. Suppose I give you the first letter of the word—P. Will you be able to supply the second?"

"R. . . ." I said without looking at her.

"Right. Now come the letter 'I'. Now you finish it."

"C and K," I enunciated hesitantly.

"There we are," she said triumphantly. "Now, I'll spell it all out and pronounce it. P, R, I, C, and K or PRICK!"

She laughed so hard that tears came to her eyes.

"Now that we know the name of the guest, how about the name of the hostess with which we are more familiar?"

"C, U, N, and T. Cunt!" I said.

"Bravo! Perfect. And what is called the act which is performed between the visitor and the hostess?" she demanded.

"F, U, C, and K. Fuck!"

"Well, I see that I was not mistaken. At least we

don't have to teach you theory, my dear Regine. What you need above all is practice, and I promise you that the Captain will give you all that you will require. Now, my love, try and get some sleep so that you can be fresh and rested tomorrow."

She gave me a cup of excellent coffee with egg yolk in it. It restored me greatly. She left. Since the movement of the ship was now less violent, I fell asleep immediately.

On waking up the next morning, you can imagine my surprise when I found myself in the arms of a completely nude man who, with a kiss, prevented the cry that was about to escape from my lips.

"Be calm, my adored Regine," he whispered, settling on top of me and nearly crushing me with his weight. "It's only your friend, the Captain. I overheard the whole conversation you had with Laura last night, and I could not resist the temptation to come and present to you my 'visitor.' Where is your hand, my dear?"

He gripped my wrist and forcibly, but not brutally, placed my hand on his member while he inserted his knees between my thighs.

"No, Captain Saint-Jean, I shall never permit that. No, I have no desire to learn how big it is. No. You will not get into me. You're hurting me. Oh!"

"Bosh. Take your hands away. You're blocking the route. Now just spread your legs a little. Oh, my sweet, let it go in," he pleaded while irresistibly shoving his prick into my cunt.

When I felt the beloved object penetrate the erogenous region and plunge into the cavern of delight, I forgot everything, kissed the sailor, and enlaced him tightly in my arms.

"How good this is, my dear. Heaven must be like this. Wiggle your backside a little. Oh, that's fine. I hope you're enjoying yourself, too," he panted as swept his organ back and forth between my inflamed labia.

"Will you let me fuck you now, my dear Regine?" he inquired, stopping his activity for a moment, but keeping his instrument firmly where it was.

"Fuck me as much as you wish and can, my dear Captain," I replied. "How can I refuse you when your handsome big prick is already stuffed into my cunt?"

My fluent usage of words like cunt, prick, and fuck made him roar with laughter. Then, with a deep sigh of satisfaction, he gushed into my burning grotto.

After lying in a swoon on my bosom for several moments, he withdrew his engine and put it back in my hand. It goes without saying that the sensation was not disagreeable and I obligingly began to stroke it.

"Regine!" the Captain explained. "You are simply delightful, and I am enchanted to have you on board. Laura and I are going to compete to see who can do the most to make the voyage pleasant for you. There is no doubt that the three of us shall amuse ourselves to our hearts' content. Now, my love, get on top of me. I want to teach you the postilion position. He placed me on him and put his hands on my buttocks. With his deft fingers, he widened the rims of my aperture and replaced the haughty head in the humid interior.

"Now, Regine, pretend that your are riding a horse, but remember to follow the movements of your mount. Giddap. How do you like that way of fucking?"

"I like it. I like it very much," I kept repeating, as I bounced up and down on his belly.

"You are doing it perfectly," he commented, straining upwards in an attempt to reach my entrails.

All of a sudden, he let out a mighty shout: "Laura, Laura! Come and look at Regine fucking me."

Laura must have been close by, for in less than half a minute, she was at our side. Without any scruples, the brazen hussy tossed off our covers, revealing my derriere in all its uncovered glory.

"Oh, Laura, you shameless thing," I screamed. "Go away, go away immediately. Release me, Captain!"

He merely clasped me all the more tightly with one hand, and with the other, he began explorations under his niece's dress. She bent over us, her nimble fingers wandering back and forth between my cunt and rear orifice. It was a game she said she named after the flower love-in-the-mist.

"Darling, don't be embarrassed by my presence. You'll get used to it in time. Besides, why are you ashamed at what I am regarding? I can see the pleasure with which your pussy is welcoming its 'visitor.' You know now, if you did not before, how variety enhances pleasure. So forward! Go on with your frolics. My being here will do nothing but arouse you the more."

"Take off your shift, Laura, and prove to Regine that you are ready for any and all sorts of amorous games."

In the twinkling of an eye, she was in the state

66

in which she entered the world and exposed the silky hair of her delightful pussy in which the Captain's hands were busily engaged. Shoving them away, she placed her mound under my nose and cried out with a joyous laugh: "Watch out, Regine." Then she divided into two her hirsute thicket and spread open the lips.

"Darling, look how red it is inside. If it could only speak, it would scream, 'Prick, prick! Give me a prick quickly. I need a prick! I need to be fucked. A fuck is what I need!!' What good is a cunt unless it is put to use? And for what purpose was it created? So, continue, Regine. On with your games!"

Inserting her finger into my slit alongside the Captain's rod, she soon caused in me a superhuman excitation.

"I'm in paradise, Laura," I murmured as I recommenced my canter. "But you just take care. I'll get my revenge."

Leaning towards me from behind, she replied: "Take it, my dear. There's nothing to stop you." At the same time, she bit my bottom cruelly just at the moment when the Captain was flooding my elated cunt and my own juice was spilling on his belly and down his thighs.

Feeling rather ashamed of myself, I hardly dared lift my eyes up to them. The Captain, dismissing his niece, took me to his cabin where he began to lovingly caress my mound.

"My little darling, you are the lucky possessor of a delicious instrument. You have given me more bliss than any woman I have ever known. Because of your noble feat, I pronounce you queen of the ship for as long as you remain aboard. All you have to do is command and you will be obeyed. Is that sufficient evidence of my devotion and adoration of you?"

"Indeed, yes," I answered as I continued rubbing his throbbing organ, "and my first queenly wish is to see you put this into my dear friend, Laura."

"Your command shall be carried out," he replied with a laugh. "I know that you are thinking of the vengeance you promised to wreak on her while diverting yourself at the same time. A double pleasure, you glutton. Well, it is an order easily carried out. What will be piquant, however, is that we are going to make use of the very weapon she had intended to employ against you."

Saying this, he opened a little chest from which he took a flexible switch adorned with green ribbons.

"Keep this and take it into your cabin. Be ready to come immediately when I call you. I am sure that Mr Yeats is on the bridge at this very moment and that Laura is flirting with him. How are we going to work it that she comes down here?" he wondered.

"I'll take care of that," I replied. "She'll soon be down here, and I'll find some excuse to take her place on the bridge."

I had more difficulties than I had anticipated in luring her below, but I did finally succeed in getting her away from Mr Yeats, whom she was treating as a declared suitor. I told her I wished to borrow a book of poetry she mentioned, and she came down with me to the salon.

I slipped into my cabin unnoticed by her. Several

moments later, I heard Laura defending her honour and speaking in a low voice to the Captain.

"Leave me alone, Uncle. I can't stay her now."

"And why not, my dear?" Captain Saint-Jean maliciously asked. "It won't be long before Yeats will have you all to himself. Indeed, he told me this morning that you have accepted his offer, and he requested my permission to marry you as soon as we land at Port-Royal in Jamaica."

"And . . . what did you say?" Laura asked in a hesitant tone.

"That he could have your hand whenever he wanted, but on one condition."

"What is that?"

"Just that he allow me to share you with him without showing any jealousy or rancour."

"Oh, Uncle, how could you have laid down such a stipulation! He will never consent, for he is a gentleman, and I know that he will hate me." Laura was near tears.

"You need have no worry on that score, my dear. Yeats and I understand each other perfectly, and we always have. I could tell you some of the adventures we have had together. He has seen me fuck his sister more than once. Now you see that you have nothing to worry about concerning the bargain we made. Let's have a little bout now, but first suck this little rascal to get him ready for action," he concluded, producing his masculinity.

"But he's waiting for me, Uncle. All right, fuck me, but let's get it over with quickly."

"Get on me horseback style. Oh, that's just right. How hot your little cunt is. Now give me a kiss," he said, lifting up her skirt over her back.

"Oh, if Regine were only here now," he

continued. "How she would relish this entrancing tableaux, a superb derriere so white and rounded, and below, a ravishing little black cunt plugged with a handsome prick. Regine, oh, Regine. Come, my darling!"

I rushed into their cabin, locking the door behind me. When Laura espied me, she smiled and said: "Your turn to enjoy the view, is it?" Then she saucily asked me: "How do you like my backside?"

"I have never seen anything lovelier. I particularly admire those adorable dimples. But it is so impudent that it should blush for shame. I think it should be punished for its immodesty. Don't you agree with me, Laura?" I inquired, brandishing the switch that I had kept hidden until that moment.

"By all means, but not too hard."

"Raise her behind, Captain. I am going to pay my debt and with interest," I ordered as I lay a few well-aimed slashes on her velvety flesh.

She gave a start and twisted in every imaginable position under the strokes of the cane.

"Bravo, Regine," exulted the Captain. "That's the way to animate her lovely little cunt. You have no idea how it's squeezing my prick. Never have I had such pleasure. Fuck! Fuck!"

Each blow on her backside seemed to give added heat and force to her pudenda.

"Oh, Regine," Laura moaned piteously, "have mercy. I can't stand it any more. Stop, I beg you! You cruel bitch, you are flaying me to pieces!"

Smarting as it was, the flagellation had its good side, for it rendered the raptures more intense and voluptuous. Laura was so excited that she was in convulsions. She rode her uncle with a fury and wriggled her buttocks in such a manner that I could see that a veritable deluge of ambrosia was about to be unloosed. It gushed forth in a series of waves, drenching their thighs and cheeks.

Heartily, the Captain applauded her valour, lovingly embraced her, and, thanking her profusely for the pleasure she had given him, admitted that his enjoyment had been considerably enhanced by the suffering she had been undergoing.

In turn, I took her in my arms while she lowered her skirts over her burning buttocks. I beseeched her to forgive me for the whipping I had given her, excusing myself by saying that I lost control of myself—the sight of her superlative derriere seemed to attract the rod irresistibly. Then I asked her to be my eternal friend.

"Of course," she managed to get out. "I pardon you. To tell the truth, the pain was more than compensated for by the raptures. Perhaps you will undergo the same experience one of these days, Regine. And I forgive you, too, my dear Uncle."

In the best of spirits, she went to rejoin Mr Yeats.

CHAPTER VI

THE CAPTAIN'S STORY

The first time that I found myself alone with Captain Saint-Jean, I requested him to tell me how he had become so intimate with his first mate.

"My dear Regine, I promised to obey your orders, and I shall do so. Here is the story. I was a very good friend of Mr Yeats's father. He and his family had boarded my ship to come and settle in the islands. William, whom I referred to as Billy, was then a lad of seventeen, and his sister, Betty, was a year his junior.

"It so happened that I was instrumental in extricating him from a bad scrape which he had got himself into.

"One day, he got drunk with some no-good characters who had the crazy idea of sneaking into the Governor's plantation and setting fire to and pillaging the buildings.

"The Governor surprised them, and placing himself at the head of a posse, he attempted to catch them. There ensued a skirmish in which one of his servants was killed. Young Billy, stunned by a blow on his head, was made prisoner, while his companions, who were the guilty ones, succeeded in making their escape.

"The Governor declared that he was going to accuse Billy of murder. You can imagine the horror and dread felt by his family.

"When I got wind of the affair, I hurried to see what I could do to help. By dint of persistence and my influence, I was able to get Billy off with a full pardon and to still the story.

"Because of this, I became an intimate friend of the family, and from that time on, whenever I was ashore on their island, I spent most of my time with them.

"Billy particularly attached himself to me. As time went on, we became inseparable. Finally, he persuaded his father to let him sign on with me. I took him on as an apprentice pilot, and ever since then, we have roved the seas together. He has passed his examinations brilliantly. Today he is a lieutenant with the promise from our shipping company of the command of his own boat.

"We have lived together and we have played together. We have shared the same perils, had the same adventures, and from this life together has resulted the intimacy that unites us.

"Like most sailors, I had a favourite woman in each port. Among them was Suzanne in Bridgetown in Barbados. She was a lovely blackeyed lass, and I was so fond of her that I never failed to see her when we touched at that port.

"On our first voyage together, Billy accompanied me when I went to visit Suzanne. Although he was eighteen years old at that time, he knew nothing whatsoever about women. Can you believe it? I tell you, Regine, that he was a virgin.

"I advised him to begin his sexual education with Suzanne and stick his unpractised member in her grotto. He was very bashful and asked me to show him how. To do him a favour, I climbed on Suzanne while he watched, and I did so in such a way that he could closely follow every detail of the operation.

"You would have split your sides with laughter if you could have seen his astonished expression when he regarded me in action. His face was purple, his eyes were glittering, and his hands were trembling. He got as close to us as he could, casting lewd looks at my organ which was functioning like a piston. He inserted his hand between us, feeling the hairy lips that were tightly embracing my prick. I was scarcely out of my lovely when he was on top of her in my place, furiously injecting his virginal virility in the hot receptacle that I had just moistened.

"In the twinkling of an eye, he ejaculated, but without giving an instant's thought to withdrawing, he undertook a second voyage to Suzanne's deep satisfaction.

"I don't have to tell you that I participated in their frolics and that my fingers were not idle during their amorous gambols.

"Ever since then, we have always had a woman in common, drawing lots to see who would be the first.

"As you can imagine, when we are at sea, we often talk about many things. Often, when we reminisce about the women we have had, we get so aroused that we masturbate each other.

"In the course of one of our conversations, I confessed to Billy that I could never look at a woman without picturing to myself her concealed charms. Excitedly, he declared that it was the same with him. Also, he admitted that he never kissed his sister Betty without thinking of her cunt. He added that once he had the good fortune to see it and kiss it. Impatiently, I demanded to know how that had come about.

"Complying with my eager request, he told me that one day while he and Betty were taking a ride in a dense part of the forest, the mare bearing his sister stumbled in a hole and threw Betty head first into a bush. Hurrying to help her up, he found her caught in the branches with her skirts over her head and her legs in the air. Through the opening in her panties, he perceived a delicious pair of lips covered with a fuzzy fleece and surrounding an opening of a deep red. Bending over her to assist her to her feet, he inadvertently pressed his face between his sister's thighs and kissed her pussy.

" 'It was so satiny and warm and it gave off such a delicious aroma. I lifted her up and stood her on her feet. Fortunately, she was not injured. We got back on our steeds and rode back home.'

"I asked him the colour of the hair he had mentioned, the hair adorning the mound. He replied that it was a superb ash blonde, and all around it was pearl-white skin and the cavern was a carmine red.

" 'Damn it, Billy. You have described Betty's centre of love so vividly that I can't wait to see it with my own eyes.'

" 'Well, why not, my old friend. I have nothing against your looking at it. I don't even mind if you fuck her, as long as you take the necessary precautions. But I don't have to tell you that. I know that you are able to give pleasure to a woman without causing her annoyances.'

"Betty came on board from time to time to visit her brother, bringing with her fruits and other delicacies. On one of these occasions, we were all drinking some punch. Betty had consumed a little more than was good for her, and she started giggling.

"Seeing her in such a condition, Billy took her in his arms and deposited her on my knees, saying: 'My dear little sister, put your arms around Saint-Jean's neck and give him a kiss. I know that you like him, and there is no doubt that he is more than just fond of you. If you do, you will make me very happy.'

"She flung her arms around my neck, pursing her seductive lips in an invitation for a kiss. After I put my lips to her, Billy did the same and interjected his knee between her legs. Then, lifting up her skirt, he took my hand and put it on her nether parts.

"At first, she did not suspect that my hand had been substituted for her brother's knee. She leaned back with her legs spread wide.

"With one of my arms, I held her by the waist, while I slid my hand down her body until it came to the opening of her panties. At the junction of the thighs and the belly, I found the sweet sanctuary I had been seeking. For a start, my fingers roamed over the *mons veneris* richly covered with its dense foliage. Descending a little more, I introduced my finger into the hot crevice as I fondled with another the rounded rims.

" 'Good heavens! Whatever are you doing? Take your hand away! If you don't, I'll scream.'

" 'Come, Betty, be nice,' interrupted Billy. 'Saint-Jean means you no harm, you know that. Permit him to keep his hand where it is. You should obey your brother!' Saying that, he opened her legs which she was trying to cross.

"Sobbing, she sprang backwards and tried once again to remove my hand. But her brother and I were convinced that she was merely putting up a show in order to have an excuse to yield. Billy cried: 'Betty, that's enough of your nonsense. If you keep on this way, I'll strip off every stitch of your clothing and leave you naked as the day you were born. We intend, the Captain and I, to examine every part of you that you keep so religiously hidden!'

" 'Oh, Billy, how can you treat me in such a shameful way. Besides, Captain Saint-Jean is married. If he wants to satisfy his carnal desires, let him go to his wife.'

" 'Don't be silly, Betty. You know how old and ugly she is. Besides, she's sick. Also, there is no time like the present.'

"Without further ado, he lifted her skirts so high that we could see unhindered the flossy fleece of her little cunt which radiated from the opening of her panties.

" 'Billy, please, put down my dress. I think I shall die of shame! Captain, I thought you had some affection and respect for me. If that is so, you would never allow my brother to disgrace me in this way.'

" 'But it is precisely because I love you, Betty, that I wanted to have a look at your adorable seat of delight. It is absolutely delicious. I never dreamed that skin could be so pearly and smooth. Why struggle any more? Your cunt has given up the battle. Let yourself go. Now you're being sensible. Your legs a little wider. Still more. Ah, perfect.'

" 'Go ahead,' she murmured in a dreamy voice. 'Do with me as you will. I am unable to defend myself against the two of you.'

"At that, she became as limp as a rag and gave up the struggle.

"Billy tenderly place her head on his lap while I slipped off her underpants down her legs.

"Oh, what seductive sight met our eyes! I could not keep my startled gaze from the flat but rounded belly, satiny and white as milk and embellished by the foliage-thick hillock. This mound was confined between two voluptuous thighs which, as they relaxed, revealed the vale of bliss.

"Insinuating my finger between these supple columns, I delicately spread them apart, and we could contemplate freely the admirable beauties of a resplendent and scintillating rosy cunt which seemed, God help me! to be aware of our greedy stares. For an eternity, we feasted our eyes on the glorious sight.

"Noticing the inflamed look with which Billy was devouring the secret beauties of his sister, I intuitively felt that the scamp would make a more intimate acquaintanceship with them before long. I was not mistaken.

" 'Well, Saint-Jean,' he triumphantly cried. 'Was my description accurate?'

" 'The reality surpasses your words, no matter how true they were. Who could ever depict such incredible beauty?'

"I bent over the incomparable venereal redoubt, whose pouting lips I ardently kissed, and darted my tongue into the half-opened crack. While I was thus engaged, Billy had unbuttoned his trousers and placed his throbbing prick between his sister's undulating posterior hemispheres. Without a moment's delay, I followed his example and inserted my impatient engine between the edges of the blessed abyss.

" 'Oh, Captain, stop that. I won't allow that.'

" 'Don't get so upset, Betty,' Billy said soothingly. 'All that's happening is that his prick is making love to your cunt.'

" 'No, Billy. That's not so. He's sticking it into me. Oh, Captain, I beg of you. Oh, you're hurting me. What are you doing to me?'

" 'I'm fucking you, my adored Betty. And I am doing so with your brother's permission for he knows that I would never do you any harm. Let's say that I am just threading your needle. Oh, my beloved. My overjoyed virility is disappearing into your cunt which is burning with love,' I exclaimed, penetrating ever deeper and making my carillons peal on her thighs.

"Overstimulated by the lascivious tableaux, Billy clutched his sister's head and shoved the head of his erect masculinity into her mouth. Then he wrapped her fingers around the rigid tube. Instinctively, Betty began to rub it back and forth. From the glitter in his eyes, I recognised the intense voluptuousness he was undergoing.

"But I felt that my moment was nearing; my sperm was going to spout. In accordance with my promise to Billy, I hastily withdrew from the danger spot. Nevertheless, I felt my prick near the orifice, running its tip across the soft fleece and inundating the mount with a copious but harmless liquid. Just at that moment, her brother's erotic reservoirs were opened, flooding her throat with a deluge of hot white nectar.

"Ever since then, the three of us have had more than one pleasant gathering. The ice was broken. She threw herself heart and soul into our rapturous games and she permitted us any sport we desired, but she was slow in granting the ultimate favour to her brother.

"Never did she refuse to let him see her in the nude, and she took obvious delight in having her bush being caressed by his lips. Many times she masturbated him or she caused his climax with her agile mouth and tongue. It was the method she generally used with him to calm his overexcited nerves when he watched us in the love act. But never until the incident I am going to tell you about did he dare to plunge his prick into her cunt. I might mention that she seemed to have had no desire for it there.

"When Betty came to visit us, she was occasionally accompanied by her chambermaid. Did she have some ulterior motive in mind? I imagine so, for the soubrette was young and winsome, and Betty quite often showed that she felt sorry that her brother did not have a partner, too. Whatever the reason, Billy quickly won the favours of the pretty lass, and I knew that after he had watched me fuck his sister, he never failed to dip his organ into the willing receptacle. He even brought her into the salon, where, with his sister watching, he took all imaginable liberties.

"By that time, Betty was the mistress of the amorous jousts, and she never had to be asked twice to take part in them, no matter what the role. At first, Betty and I had to hold the maid down while Billy got on top of her.

"After the usual preliminaries, we stripped the neophyte from head to toe and then did the same to Betty. Billy and I were then in the same state of undress.

"Rugs and cushions were scattered on the floor where we indulged in the most unbridled *parties carrées*. Derrieres and faces did not remain in the same position longer than a few seconds.

"One time, Billy proposed that we blindfold the two girls so that they could not see what we were going to do. The suggestion was agreed to, and the scapegrace whispered that I should have my pleasure with the young maid by way of a change. Regine, you have no idea of what pleasure a new cunt is for a man. There is no more irresistible attraction. Consequently, you can imagine with what eagerness I accepted the generous offer. Immediately straddling my victim, I had it in her to the bottom with a mere three jabs.

" 'There's no need for hurry, Billy,' I cried. 'Here we are on the second or third round, and we are going to have more fun than we ever had before.'

"As I said that, I stuck my tongue in Betty's mouth while I slowly dangled my tool in the soubrette's moist crevice.

" 'That suits me to a T, old friend,' answered Billy. Passing his hand under my buttocks, for we were side by side, he grabbed my testicles and ground them so lasciviously that, flushed as they were, they spurted their copious contents through the swollen tube into a cunt more than grateful to receive them.

"Shortly after that, we had to set sail again. The

last time I saw Betty, she had become the wife of an old but wealthy planter by the name of Hobbs. She's the lady you know as Lizzy, whom your father fucks every chance he can get.

"Now you understand the reason for the close friendship between my first mate and self. And also you recognise I was not insulting Laura in the slightest when I made the sharing of her a condition of my permission for her marriage.

"I have told you everything and answered all your questions. I deserve my reward, and let it be my prick intoxicating itself in your adored cunt."

CHAPTER VII

THE STORY OF LAURA

Although she was very preoccupied with the preparations for her nuptials, Laura did not forget our mutual promise to exchange confidences. She assured me that if I wished to tell her how I had been initiated into the pleasures of love, she would reciprocate.

I needed very little persuasion, and recounted to her my first childish endeavours with Dick and his ultimate triumph. Then I depicted to her the scenes in the correction room, details about old Mr Snigger and the girls he chastised, and told her about the affair between my father and Mrs Hobbs, Lieutenant Yeats's sister.

In spite of the fact that she had already had some inkling of these matters, Laura was greatly amused by my recital.

When I finished, I urged her to keep her end of the bargain, which she willingly did.

"As you know, Regine, I began very early. You probably have heard that my mother was the sister of Captain Saint-Jean and was married to a doctor. She died when I was only fourteen years old, and my father remarried.

"We were very poor at that time and our home was nothing but a tiny shanty. We were so cramped for space that my bed was at the foot of my parents' and all that separated us was a curtain.

"Often at night when I was unable to sleep, I heard their bed squeak in a most peculiar fashion, and, more than one time, I heard them whisper to each other things like this: 'Now you can go ahead.' 'Take it in your hand.' 'Put it inside yourself.' 'Lift up your legs.' 'Don't let it go.' 'Squeeze it between your fingers.' And lots of other things. Then there were jolts, bumps, and pants, in the midst of which my father gave out long sighs and moans that were so passionate. Sometimes my stepmother warned him in a low voice: 'Be careful! Don't make so much noise. Be quiet. You'll wake up the little one.'

"Other times, I heard Papa make her say the words, 'prick, cunt, and fuck,' and force her to tickle his backside, to stroke his organ, to cuddle his testicles, and even to let him have her in the rear.

"At that period in my life, I did not know the exact meaning of those words and expressions that I had just heard, but I had a vague idea of what they referred to. You can imagine how attentive I was to the slightest sound and word. But my overpowering desire was to witness what they were doing.

"It goes without saying that it would not be easy. As a rule, it was after they had gone to bed and the room was plunged into absolute darkness that they began their games. For a long time, I was unable to satisfy my curiosity.

"Nevertheless, one bright spring morning, I had the good luck to wake up just at the moment when they were engaged in their sport. I heard my father speak. 'Lift up your behind so I can look at your cunt while you suck my prick.'

"Quickly, but with the greatest caution for fear of being caught, I drew aside the curtain slightly. My stepmother was on her knees. Her spread-open legs imprisoned my father on whose face she shamelessly rested her enormous white derriere.

"She was leaning forward, supporting herself on her elbows. In her hand, she was holding a sort of long fleshy roller which, surrounded by a thick scrub of black hair, protruded from Papa's belly.

"That instrument, the first of which it was my pleasure to contemplate, held my attention for a considerable time. It fascinated me and I could not turn my eyes away from it.

"I noticed that it was tipped with a kind of large purplish head which my stepmother rubbed back and forth between her lips and nose while her hand ran up and down the tube itself. After several moments, she took a good portion of it in her mouth and began to suck it greedily.

" 'How grateful I am for the bliss you are giving me,' my father gasped. 'My prick is in seventh heaven.'

"Oh, what good luck! Now I knew the meaning of the word 'prick.'

"Now, get down lower!' my father continued. 'It's my turn to place my lips on your cunt and make *minette* to you.'

"Well, I now knew what a cunt was.

"Excited by what I saw, I lowered my hand to my little hole, and as I gingerly touched it in a state of stupefaction, I wondered if I ever would have a cunt as large and hairy as my stepmother's.

"While I was engrossed in such reflections, Papa

opened with his two hands his wife's thighs and began ardently to suck the cunt. She did not stop rubbing his rod which was as hard as iron.

"That went on for some time until Papa suddenly said: 'And now, let's fuck.'

"Then, making his wife remain in the position I have described, that is to say, resting on her elbows and knees, he got behind her, spread her legs, opened the flaps of the cunt, and regarded the gaping cavity which resembled an oversized mouth eager to devour something.

"Grabbing his prick, he worked the head into the hole and then gave it a violent jab. His arms were enlaced around his partner's haunches, and with quick movements of his loins, he directed his utensil backwards and forwards between the two hair-covered lips.

"The tableau enabled me to understand the meaning of the word 'fuck'.

"But I could not understand that my stepmother obviously was experiencing no pain from the way she was groaning.

" 'How good that feels. Shove! Shove it in harder! Give me everything you have, Harry. It is so wonderful when you fuck me from behind. It is such a marvellous sensation to feel your belly on my backside. Hold me tighter. Put your finger there, on my button.'

"Both were sighing and letting out voluptuous inarticulate sounds. All of a sudden, she sank down as in a faint. Without taking out his prick, Papa flopped on her and continued what he was doing.

"From that time on, I never ceased spying on their erotic tourneys, and I soon became familiar with their lascivious positions and licentious words.

I participated in their games by masturbating in rhythm with their bounces on the bed. Within a short time, my finger was able to penetrate my little hole without giving me any pain.

"In the meanwhile, my stepmother fell ill, and it was necessary to keep her in isolation. I was relegated to another room, which was a blessing for me. Now that I was free to play with myself as much as I wanted, I overdid it. As you know, excessive indulgence in this pastime can be disastrous for a young girl's health. My condition began to deteriorate, and I learned to moderate my desires.

"Until I was sixteen, nothing eventful or of interest occurred except that a silky floss began to adorn my *mons veneris*.

"I went to school regularly, and since I liked to study, I sought to broaden my knowledge as much as possible.

"One fine day, there came to our school a new French teacher. His name was Louis Martel. A handsome fellow he was with a fine bearing. And he was young. I don't have to tell you that we girls fell in love with him on first sight.

"The new instructor outwardly was rather stiff and formal. And he paid no particular attention to any of us. He was conscientious in his duties and seemed to have other preoccupations than being a good teacher.

"Among his pupils, I was the most attentive and industrious. For that reason, he seemed to have a warm spot in his heart for me and he encouraged me in my studies. I responded to his attention with renewed efforts, realising his good will and attempting to please him in any way I could.

"Little by little, I began to have a genuine affection for him and to me it seemed that it was returned. Often, his arm absent-mindedly grazed mine, and, during class, his eyes rarely wandered from mine.

"Also, I noticed that the protuberance outlined on the crotch of his trousers seemed to grow bigger when he spoke to me, and, particularly, when he looked at me. Once, by accident, I leaned on it with my elbow, and it seemed to give a convulsive leap at the touch.

"As for myself, it was as if an electric charge was racing through my veins. My nerves were on edge, my blood was boiling, and I felt sexual emanations. My mind was filled with the thought of his prick. I saw it everywhere. Every object I viewed assumed its shape and form. At night, I dreamed about it, and, on several occasions, I woke up suddenly in the middle of the night imagining that I was holding Louis in my arms and that his organ was penetrating me.

"Now I began to take an increasing interest in studying my pussy. With the aid of a mirror placed between my legs, I examined it, asking myself what Louis would think of it, if he would like to put his prick into it and fuck me.

" 'Oh, if only I could show it to him,' I wailed. 'I am sure he would become inflamed and he would not be so formal with me.'

"During this period of my infatuation, we had an unexpected school holiday, and it was decided that we, teachers and students, would go and pick mangoes in a nearby grove.

"Once there, we divided into small groups. How did that come about? I don't know. But whatever the reason, Louis Martel and I found ourselves alone, separated and far from the others. He took my basket, saying he would carry it while I picked the fruit. We started off looking for the right trees, getting farther and farther away from the others. Nevertheless, our isolation was far from displeasing to either of us, and we were not afraid.

"We did not fill my basket quickly. My mind was not on mangoes, and for his part, Monsieur Martel was busying in disentangling my skirts that got caught in the underbrush or in helping me free myself from the brambles that impeded my progress. But we merely laughed and joked at these difficulties. Finally, we came across a very large tree whose branches were sagging down under the weight of the fruit.

" 'At last,' I cried. 'Here's a tree that is easy to climb and loaded with what we have been looking for.' I got up on one of the lowest branches. 'I'll pick the mangoes, Monsieur Martel, and throw them down to you. In turn, you'll catch them and put them in the basket.'

" 'Fine!' he agreed. 'Only watch out so that you don't fall.'

"He took up his post while I climbed above his head. I noted that his eyes were following me. Suddenly, there popped into my head the thought that this was the ideal occasion to give him a glimpse of my secret charms. I made up my mind then and there to take advantage of it and see what effect it would have on him.

"I scrambled from branch to branch, spreading my legs as wide as I could. It was a sweltering hot day, and I was not wearing any underpants. Also, my petticoat was very short. It seemed to me that he could not fail to regard my thighs as well as the rosy slit between them, the narrow crevice on which the fleece was starting to sprout.

"Slyly looking at him below, I could make out that his face had turned scarlet and that his eyes were glittering with an unaccustomed fire.

" 'It is harder than I thought to get to the fruit,' I called down to him. 'I think I have to go a bit farther out on the branch.'

" 'Watch out, Laura. That branch does not seem very strong and I doubt if it can bear your weight.'

"Scarcely had he uttered this warning than a crack and a scream made themselves heard while the branch and I came tumbling down. Louis caught me in his arms before I hit the ground. The fall was not very hard, but he was so directly under me that my skirts covered his head and my derriere landed right on his face. In spite of everything, I was slightly stunned.

"When I came to, I found myself stretched out on the grass and Monsieur Martel kneeling at my side, chaffing my hands. He seemed very agitated, his face was scarlet, and I gathered that he had examined my concealed charms while I was in the swoon. To tell the truth, the thought made me blush and I was not a little embarrassed.

" 'Oh, Mademoiselle Laura, how happy I am to see that you are all right. There's nothing seriously wrong, I trust.'

" 'No, it's nothing.' I assured him as I tried to get to my feet. 'Oh, I must have scraped my knee, because it hurts when I rest on it.'

" 'Permit me to see if there is any swelling,' he said worriedly.

" 'Please do so,' I answered as I raised my skirt.

He ran his hand over my knee, touching it all over.

" 'There doesn't seem to be anything the matter, although it feels a little hot. Would you like me to massage it while you rest for a few moments?'

" 'I would be most grateful,' I said as I extended my leg.

"He began to rub gently my knee and up to where my thighs began. Gradually, his hand mounted and kept going higher. It finally stopped, as if by mistake, on my downy mound over which his hand ran tenderly. Since I did not appear angry at the liberty he had taken, he boldly took complete possession of it. His fingers started to caress my labia and clitoris.

" 'Monsieur Martel!' I exclaimed in mock indignation. 'Remove your hand and allow me to get up.'

" 'My dearest Laura, do let me tell you how much I adore you. I am head over heels in love with you!' he declared passionately, taking me by the waist and reclining me on the grass again. 'This ravishing little nest, so mossy and moist, is unbelievably seductive. Please permit me to touch it and look at it a little. Just a little.'

"Saying that, he lifted up my skirts and insinuated himself between my legs.

" 'Oh, Louis, stop that,' I said sternly. 'Your moustache is tickling me. How is it possible that you like to kiss me on that spot?'

" 'How is it possible?' he repeated in a wondering tone. 'Simply because it is the most ravishing little cunt I have ever seen. It is made to be kissed and sucked. If it were permitted to insert something nice in there, what a delicious pleasure it would experience. Do you know what I am referring to, Laura?'

" 'I haven't the faintest idea, Louis,' I lied. 'But tell me how, if something were inserted in it, I would have so much bliss?'

" 'Because of this, my love,' he answered, placing in my hand a magnificent instrument standing at haughty attention which he had produced from his trousers.

" 'Oh, Louis, I can't even bear to look at it, I am so ashamed. But just to please you, I'll hold it and stroke it a little. Would you like that?'

" 'My darling, there are no words to express the delight you are bestowing on me. By the way, Laura, do you know the name of the thing you are holding?'

" 'How should I know?' I replied, lying again. "You tell me what it is, my dear professor.'

" 'It's called a prick. Laura, repeat the word. Say it! Prick!'

" 'Prick . . . dear little prick,' I dutifully said. 'Louis, does every man have an instrument like yours, a prick?' I wanted to know.

" 'Yes, indeed, my darling. Every man has one. The only thing is that some are big and others are small. The sizes and shapes vary. But long and skinny or thick and short, no matter what the dimensions are, all pricks are designed for the same purpose.'

" 'And what are they used for?' I asked with a laugh.

" 'To overwhelm all girls and women by penetrating their cunts,' he answered solemnly.

" 'Really? How curious. And do girls let men do that?'

" 'Do they let men do that?' he echoed with a shocked voice. 'What is a cunt for, tell me? That soft and slippery passage is the natural home for a prick where it can move about. If you only had an idea, Laura, what voluptuousness it causes. Please let me fuck you. Oh, don't resist. There's nobody here. We cannot be seen and you will be thrilled no end.'

" 'Oh, no. I can't let you right now. No!' I protested. 'I'm too afraid. Perhaps another time. Later!'

"But Louis was not stupid enough to let such a propitious moment slip by. Without bothering to ask my permission any more, he took his position between my legs which he raised. Then he pushed the head of his rod between the lips of my vagina. I told myself that since he had got that far, the best course was to facilitate his task as best I could.

"His prick was of reasonable proportions. The rounded big head completely plugged the opening. By that time, I was so impatient and eager to have it in me that, oblivious to the pain, I shoved myself upwards against him as hard as I could. In his efforts to clear a passage, he could not hold back his semen and he discharged. The result was that he was immobilised for a moment, but the liquid, escaping from his prick, greased the duct. Having quickly regained its former vigour, the weapon shot forward victoriously and was in complete possession of my burning interior. Never before in my life had I experienceed such raptures.

"The exhilarated Louis commenced again that come and go movement that we prize so highly, we women, and he asked me what sort of a sensation I experienced when I was being fucked.

" 'Oh, Louis, it is out of this world. It is divine. It is impossible to describe the joy I have when I feel your prick go back and forth between the flaps of my cunt. My nerves are set on edge and seem about to break. You drive me out of my mind!'

"I was not exaggerating. Indeed, this first intercourse gave me a strange intense pleasure that I never expected. Since you have experienced that bliss yourself, I don't have to define to you the transports you have when a prick is stuck into you for the first time. And you know, too, that frenzy that takes possession of you during the final thrusts which get faster and faster. And then there is that supreme prostration you undergo while the copious sperm inundates and boils you. Isn't it so. Regine, that the only way you can know what it is like is to experience it?

"The pleasure that both Louis and I enjoyed was the keenest. He and I felt afterwards as if we had been broken on the rack. For several minutes, we lay side by side on the grass. We were motionless except for our hands which were as busy as ever. His continued to stimulate my slit and excite again my clitoris, while mine toyed with his member and cuddled his testicles.

"My lover was indefatigable. Within a short time, his organ stood up more proudly and rigidly than before. It was all ready for a new assault.

"Throwing me on my back, Louis lifted my skirts again up to the navel, placed his head between my legs, and with a sort of fury, did *minette* and the rose-leaf to me, devouring my cunt and ass-hole with raging ardour. As if it were the most natural thing in the world, I began to suck his prick and inserted my finger in his tiny rear little hole. We

94

looked like the figure sixty-nine, and I later learned that that is what our position is called. The exercise pleased him very much, as you can well believe, and while I was busy sucking him, he had only one preoccupation, and that was to make me discharge. He was so adept and skilful with his fingers and tongue that the wished-for moment was not long in coming. His lips were pressed tightly to my cunt. One would have thought he was attempting to drink all of me. Embracing me with renewed vigour, he declared that tasting my liquid flow between his lips drove him absolutely mad with pleasure.

"Before we knew it, an hour had passed in these delightful and varied games. Louis took advantage of it to prove himself an adept and fervent devotee of the Paphian cult and to initiate me into some of the rites and ceremonies of life.

"Nevertheless, it was time to come to our senses and rejoin our companions whom we had neglected too long. We got up and I tried to walk, but my knee, more badly sprained than I had thought, refused to function. Consequently, Louis found himself obliged to carry me in his arms the greater part of the way. But with the gallantry that characterises the men of his nation, he averred that his burden seemed much less heavy now that he knew what incomparable treasures his load consisted of.

"I answered him with an impassioned kiss and hugged him ever more tightly around his neck.

"I had to spend an entire week at home, and, of course, I could not attend classes. Louis came to see me every day, and since he spent at least an hour alone with me while I was reclining on an easy-chair in the garden, I had nothing to complain about.

"One of my school-mates who was very close to me also visited me as often as she could.

"She was a young girl of rare beauty with russet hair and wide blue eyes. She was held up to all the other girls as a model of modesty and seemliness, but we, all promising young spies, knew better and gave her the nickname of Miss Hypocrite.

"She was quick to spot the intimacy that existed between Monsieur Martel and myself, and she seemed to take a close interest in it. Since she noted that I liked to talk and hear about Louis, she usually turned the conversation to that subject.

"Also, it appeared that she made it a point to show up each time that my friend was coming or leaving, although she pretended that she was going when he and I were chatting. Once, she concealed her presence so successfully that without our knowledge she was able to witness a particularly passionate amorous session.

"As usual, as soon as Louis was at my side, I undid the buttons of his trousers, pulled down his suspenders, and took possession of his throbbing love organ. After cuddling and kissing it, I took the dazzling head into my mouth as I fondled his balls and patted his backside.

"Repaying me in like coin, Louis had run his hands between my thighs and titillated tenderly the sensitive aperture. Then placing me on my knees, he tucked my skirts, revealed my derriere, and then began to fuck in the dog manner.

"We were at the height of our excitement. Puffing with pleasure, Louis, in order to prolong the bliss, slowed his tempo. It seemed that his beloved masculinity was swimming around in my grotto. I expressed my supreme raptures with little inarticulate cries and, in order to stimulate our already overheated sensations even more, I uttered all the words of love that come to my mind.

"All of a sudden, Miss Hypocrite, whether because she could no longer restrain her ardour or because she was jealous of my gratification which she was not sharing, appeared behind us.

"Startled, Louis stopped, withdrew his member that was just about to flood me with his heady liquid, abandoned my parched cunt, and stared furiously at the intruder. But as soon as he recognised her, his alarm turned to mirth and he let out a joyous whoop.

" 'Well, well, so it's Mademoiselle Hypocrite. Since you have caught us *in flagrante delicto*, you are going to join us for your pleasure and for ours.'

"Much to my surprise, she made little or no resistance. My lover embraced her without her putting up any opposition. She let his hand wander up beneath her skirts which he lifted. Then he exposed her cunt and turning her on her back, he mounted her.

" 'Just take a look at Mademoiselle Hypocrite's cunt, Laura,' he shouted, pointing out with his finger two plump rounded lips abundantly covered with reddish down.

"His eyes sparkled and glitterd while he greedily took in the uncovered treasure, all the more attractive because of its freshness and novelty.

" 'I hope you are not going to be jealous, my dear Laura,' he cried exultantly. 'Come, you put your old friend into Mademoiselle Hypocrite's hole.'

"He placed in my hand the member quivering at the prospect of a new target and a new joust.

"I could not but help share his enthusiasm when I contemplated the rutilant conniceties of my schoolmate. Making the best of it, I did as I was asked and adjusted the head of his engine on the half-opened flaps.

"I fixed a curious eye on her. The slimy crevice seemed to be burning with ardent desire while Louis, having regained his pristine vigour, was straining to make his way into it.

"To their mutual mortification, the passage remained inviolate.

" 'Shove harder!' I yelled at Louis as I squeezed his testicles.

"Hypocrite shut her eyes. Nearly fainting and ready to scream at the energetic efforts my lover was making to introduce his member but determined to stifle any sound, she tremblingly clutched the hem of her skirt, shoved it in her mouth and furiously began to bite it.

"It seemed that my interior was a blazing furnace.

" 'Pull it out! Pull it out!' I loudly ordered Louis. 'I'm going to moisten your weapon in my mouth.'

" 'No, no, Louis, don't take it out. I beg you. I can bear the pain. Push harder. Still more. Oh, I feel it going in,' cried Hypocrite.

"With a convulsive upward jab, she succeeded in breaking down the last obstacle.

"Now the prick was safely nestled in the lower depths, which threatened to swallow up the intruder entirely.

"A simultaneously uttered barely audible sigh from their lips betrayed their mutual bliss. For the first time, the voracious gland that was under my eyes was feasting itself on the delicious prey that Mother Nature provided for its use and delectation.

"Although I was not enjoying a rapture equal to theirs, I did partially share in their joys. Contentedly, I regarded that magnificent prick imprisoned in the newly opened cavern.

"The adhesive labia were glued all round the intrusive weapon. With an oddly lascivious suction power, the lips seemed to wish to hold it back when he retreated for a renewed attack. Her buttocks appeared to be guests at the banquet. At each thrust, they opened and then slowly and voluptuously closed as the dangling testicles struck and bounced off them.

"Louis had ejaculated almost as soon as he had plunged his member in the glowing receptacle. But he was so enthusiastic about a new instrument to perform on and Miss Hypocrite so willing to oblige that he returned for a new charge almost immediately and made her faint again in a wave of amorous semen.

"It was over for me. With the appearance of the new gem, the old had to disappear.

"It did not take me long to detect a sudden change in Louis's attitude and manner toward me. He avoided me when he could, and he made it plain that he no longer found in my arms the pleasure he had once enjoyed.

"From that bitter experience I learned how fickle men can be. Also, I found that a new cunt—simply because it is new—is enough to create an aversion to what was once so eagerly sought and adored.

"Fortunately, I was philosophical and young enough to take it in stride and not tear my heart out. But I had tasted of the delights of sexual pleasure, and far from renouncing them, I had but one goal, and that was to go as far as I could with them. At that point, I made the firm determination not to let any occasion for it escape.

"There were not lacking young men as handsome as Louis who, I knew, would have been overjoyed to obtain my favours. They were only waiting for a chance to pay me court or some encouragement on my part. One of them was a youth by the name of Bertie whom I often encountered at our dances. To my mind, he seemed just right for my designs. Moreover, his manners were impeccable, a point on which I lay great stress.

"I could see that he was enterprising and resolute, and I decided that I would meet him halfway by not rejecting his advances, no matter how audacious they may have been.

"One evening at a ball after we had danced several times together, he led me without protest on my part into the vestibule. From there we went upstairs to a secluded nook where we could rest free from snooping eyes.

"Once ensconced there, he put his arm around my waist, gave me a warm kiss, took my hand, and impudently placed it on his organ still jailed in his trousers.

" 'My dear, sweet Laura,' he said in a tone that was both decisive and timid, 'I don't know why it is, but every time that I am near you, and especially when I touch you, as, for example, when I squeeze your hand, this part of my body stands up and swells. It is most uncomfortable and embarrasses me. As a matter of fact, it even hurts, and I don't know what to do about it. You are kind and intelligent. Please give me your advice. See if you can come up with a remedy."

" 'Oh, that, Bertie,' I exclaimed. 'Whatever in the world are you asking me? You are sadly mistaken, my dear boy. I'm not a doctor. If you need advice, why don't you go and see my father? Perhaps he can find a cure for your malady.'

"Instead of replying to my suggestion, he began to fumble with my skirts. I played the innocent.

" 'I assure you, Bertie, that I have nothing in my pocket except my handkerchief. Don't you believe me? Look for yourself. But, Bertie, that's not my pocket. It's the slit of my skirt and you have no business in there. No decent young lady would let a man put his hand in there!'

" 'Dearest Laura, why are you so cruel and hard-hearted,' he complained. 'It is there, the remedy that I so desperately need. Tell me, don't you have somewhere around there another tiny little pocket? All I need is to touch the edges of it. Oh, now I feel it. How lovely it is! It reminds me of a pure white satin. But how hot it is! It is burning. May God forgive me, but, Laura, you are having an orgasm. Quickly, now. Stand up and come over here.'

"Saying that, he almost dragged me towards an open door nearby.

" 'No, no,' I protested. 'We could be surprised. Someone could come. No, no!'

" 'You don't have to worry about that,' he assured me. 'I can promise you that nobody will come in here. The room is mine for the night and we'll be in there just for a few minutes.'

"He slammed the door shut, latched it, and then tumbled me on a bed that I had not noticed in the dim light of the candle. He sat me on the couch and tried to force me on my back as he put my hand on his vibrating virility.

" 'Just feel how it is burning, Laura,' he said pleadingly. 'Oh, my love, have pity on me. It is on the verge of exploding, and only your curing tiny cunt can assuage its pain. Do let me put it inside of you. Oh, Laura, you will be enchanted at the sensation.'

" 'No! No!' I adamantly refused. 'I don't want to. Besides, you would hurt me, and Bertie, just think of the possible consequences.'

" 'Have no fear on that score,' he replied reassuringly. 'I won't hurt you. On the contrary. As for the possibly disagreeable results, it's merely a question of knowing how to go about it. Ah, what a kind-hearted and merciful girl you are. Now just widen your legs a little. That's just right.'

"Stretching me out on the bed, he placed my legs on his shoulders, thrust his gland into my crevice, and holding me firmly on his shoulders, he commenced his assault.

"His prick was enormous. In comparison, Louis's was nothing but a child's toy. Try to picture it to yourself, Regine. I was leading him to believe that he was plucking a maidenhead, and I squeezed my thighs together as tightly as I could. I imagine you won't be surprised when I tell you that he had the greatest difficulty getting it into me.

" 'How tight you are, Laura,' he exclaimed in surprise. "Oh, please, help me, or I won't be able to breach your virginal barricade.'

"Laughing up my sleeve, I did my best to confirm him in his erroneous thinking.

" 'Oh, Bertie,' I squealed in feigned fright.

'Please do stop. Your instrument is hurting me something terrible and I won't be able to stand it much longer.'

"I pretended to elude his embrace. But my resistance, and such was my intention, only served to stoke his flames. Holding me still more firmly, he redoubled his efforts.

"Soon I felt the cherished plaything make progress, enter the passage, distend the tissues of my flesh, and cause my nerves to quiver with anticipation. Just for form's sake, I let out a little scream, but being sensible, I thought I had defended my honour sufficiently. Consequently, I abandoned myself completely, widening the space between my legs as much as I could in order not to lose an iota of what he could give me.

" 'My sweetest Laura,' he murmured ecstatically. 'Just forget about the pain. It is just once and then it will never return. The bliss will more than make up for it. Is it not as wonderful as I promised? Laura, I feel it coming. Hold me more tightly in your arms. This is the moment. Hold tight, darling. Take it all, dearest. Take all I have.'

"His boiling seed swept into my parched cunt, throwing me into a delirium of delight. Disregarding the possible consequences, I held him imprisoned between my legs until his prick had expended the last drop of his ambrosia into the very bottom of me.

"I had forgotten myself completely in my raptures, although I was aware of the terrible risk I was running. But I did not care. I had to savour the experience to the full. Not for anything in the world would I have missed that overpowering delight of which men often frustrate us, as you know, my dear, when suddenly they take out the instrument just at the moment we feel that it is about to touch the heart.

"I held him passionately close to me. My cunt was greedily sucking in his prick while my backside convulsively wiggled. Soon I felt his rod stiffening again. To arouse him again, I whispered encouraging words into his ear.

" 'Oh, again, again, again. Oh, Bertie, my love. Fuck me! Fuck me once again. I'll say anything you want. Cunt. Prick. Ass-hole. Tits. Balls. Oh, Bertie, fuck me. I am mad for your prick to fuck me time and time again. Shove it all the way in. Courage! Give me it all, every drop of your precious sperm.'

"Our transports were frenzies. Our derrieres were bobbing up and down like corks in a stormy sea. His humid testicles clung to my buttocks. Finally, our liquids blended as our bodies performed a St Vitus dance. And as we fell back in a swoon, we were still enwrapped in each other's arms.

"When we came back to our senses and stood up. I realised how mussed and rumpled my hair and dress were.

" 'Just look what you have done to me,' I said to him accusingly. " 'How can I go back to the ball looking like this?'

" 'Don't worry, my love. I'll go down and tell our hostess that you are indisposed and wish to return home. We'll leave without anyone seeing us.'

"Without waiting for my reply, he disappeared and returned promptly bearing my wrap and a bottle of champagne.

"In my state of stimulation and fever, the wine was most welcome and we quickly emptied the bottle. I have to admit that I consumed more than my due share.

"Now reinvigorated, although my head was slightly swimming, I was ready for any adventure. Boldly holding my new lover around the waist, I disappeared with him into the gloom!'

CHAPTER VIII

CONTINUATION AND END OF LAURA'S STORY

"Shortly afterwards, we met another merry fellow who had one of the most suggestive and droll names imaginable. He was called Toplady, but his nickname was Topsy and he was known as such to everybody. Bertie and he were old friends, and everybody knew that the two of them had enjoyed a thousand joyous pranks and adventures.

"Normally, I would have slipped off to bed alone, but overstimulated by the champagne and perspiring freely, I had only the faintest idea of what I was doing.

"Consequently, when Topsy was seized by the whim to kiss me, clasp me around the waist while I was being supported by Bertie, to up my skirts, and explore thoroughly my cunt and derriere, I made not the slightest resistance. Encouraged by my apathy, the fellow's insolence knew no bounds. Pulling down my panties, he planted his weapon right in the centre of the inviting target and declared that he was going to have me right on the spot.

"Bertie, however, restrained him, telling him: 'Not so fast, old fellow. A little patience. And put back in your muscle. We'll find a more suitable place in a jiffy.'

"Each taking me by an arm, we proceeded to the seamier quarter of the city and stopped before a squalid house.

"I did not like the look of things, and I asked them to take me back home as they had promised.

" 'Not just yet, my dear,' said Bertie. 'There's no hurry. The ball will last for another hour at least, and it would be stupid not to use this time in having some amusement. There is nothing to worry about, so please don't worry, Laura. You know you can rely on me to see that you get back home safe and sound at the right time.'

"Carrying me in his robust arms, he climbed a flight of steps in front of the structure and deposited me at the entrance. Topsy, striking a match, lit a candle and then led us into a large chamber mostly furnished with low big divans. Only later did I find out that we were in a real brothel.

"There was a large table in the centre of the room, and on it rested a candelabra which Topsy illuminated. While he was doing that, Bertie dumped me on one of the sofas in such a manner that my skirts flew up. Then he addressed Topsy.

" 'There you are, my friend. Now's the time and the place. I'm making you a gift that is truly out of the ordinary and one that I know you'll appreciate. For once in your life, forget your coarse instincts and give the young lady a good gentlemanly fuck. Remember that she is a girl of breeding whom you have in your arms, you swine, and not one of your usual sows. To prove it, look at that cunt. Is it not

107

worthy of a queen? Fix your eyes on those luscious lips. See how they jut out. Don't you see how lickerish and appetising they are? And what do you have to say about that fleece? There exists in the world none that is so soft and downy. I could go on forever enumerating her beauties. How about the red valley that so gently meanders in its midst? Do you smell that aromatic odour? Now what do you think, you old fucker?'

" 'It is absolutely stunning, ripping!' Topsy gasped in admiration. Plunging his head between my thighs, he started to titillate my seat of desire with his tongue, licking the contours and pushing hard into the passage. Then opening the lips wider, he inserted his tongue as deep as he could. I experienced an ineffable pleasure.

"Bertie, in the meantime, had put his gland in my hand. The contact of this beloved glowing morsel made me all the more tipsy. Gluttonously, I took it in my mouth and lasciviously sucked it while massaging it with my lips.

"All of a sudden, Topsy sprang up, striking his forehead with his fist. 'I have an idea,' he cried.

" 'That's great,' Bertie said. 'Tell us about it.'

" 'Lie on your back with Laura on top of you on her knees. Good. Fine. Now put your prick in her cunt. Now, for my turn. I'll mount both of you and fuck wherever I can!'

"Bertie began to laugh. 'Let's give it a try, my old friend. I see what you have in mind. Go ahead, Laura. You'll have twice the voluptuousness and I'll see to it that no harm comes to you.'

"The pair promptly set to work stripping off my clothes until I was almost completely nude. At first, I did not like that at all. But when I saw Bertie stretched out on his back and his proud organ standing erect, I hurled myself on him without waiting to be invited. Following Topsy's instructions, I placed the inflated member at the entrance to the redoubt which was ready to receive it and gently pressed myself against it. Its rigidity penetrating me, it soon filled my hollow with its comforting warmth. Urged on by the instinct for pleasure, I began to wiggle lasciviously up and down until Bertie stopped me.

" 'Take it easy, my dear,' he said. 'Wait until our good friend Topsy is in you, too. Then all three of us will go into action.'

"At that moment, Topsy was engaged in carefully scrutinising my cunt and derriere.

"I was naive enough to believe that he was simply going to try and insert his prick in the same hole where Bertie's was already lodged. Instead, the blackguard grabbed me by the haunches, and before I realised what he was doing, he had his prick into the well-greased aperture of my derriere, in which he began to vigorously fuck me.

"On the entrance of his oversized gland into such a tight orifice, I felt a sharp stab of almost unbearable pain. But once it cleared the first barrier and the head was in, and then the whole rod, then . . . Oh, Regine, you have no idea of my bliss. I was in seventh heaven.

"The interplay of those two pricks so close to each other was so stimulating and lascivious. Simultaneously, I felt the slap of Bertie's belly on mine and the smack of Topsy's on my buttocks while the latter's lubricated gland was reaching down to my entrails.

"Try as I might, Regine, I can give you with

words no idea of the indescribable ecstasy. I would have cheerfully given up the ghost at that moment.

"Suddenly, at the peak of our erotic transports, we heard steps on the staircase, and before we had time to disengage, two partially naked men accompanied by two young women as little garbed as they, stumbled into the chamber.

"Taking in the tableau with a sweeping glance, the newcomers told Bertie and Topsy not to worry about them and to continue our joyous frolics. Having reassured us, the two couples formed a group around us.

"Without the slightest sense of shame, the men waved their swollen organs back and forth near my face while the two girls caressed and stroked the two pricks paying homage to my two orifices.

"As for myself, I had reached such a state of concupiscence that I insanely clutched the two new virilities and greedily brought them to my lips.

"What follies the grape causes us to commit! What inexplicable fantasies and aberrations the venereal rutting leads us to!

"Then before me were two individuals with sinister appearances whom, ordinarily, I would have avoided speaking to and having any contact with. In fact, I would have hurried by them if I had met them on the street. Yet those two men were regaling me with their vibrating members crowned with enormous flamboyant diadems. There was no doubt that they had just emerged from the dubious interiors of the two street girls. Well, those pricks, not only did I regard them without displeasure, but I actually delighted in them with my eyes. What joy their touch gave me! I became intoxicated from their odour. I sucked them alternately as I stroked them and felt within me the spasmodic movements of the pricks inserted in my front and rear. Now they seemed welded into one unbending bar fucking and meeting in the same passage.

"While this was going on, the two strange girls were continuously licking us and stroking us as they rubbed their cunts against one another with complete nonchalance.

"The erotic folly had reached its peak. All of us began to yell at the same time. It was a veritable outburst of lewd words. Ass. Cunt. Prick. Masturbate. Fuck. Suck. Kiss. Bugger. Piss. In the midst of this clamour, the floodgates of voluptuousness were opened wide, releasing torrents of sperm.

"After a short pause to recuperate, it was decided that one of the girls was going to be whipped.

"With the promise of not carrying matters to extremes and a substantial indemnity for her trouble, one agreed to lie on her stomach with her bottom raised into the air.

"To give her courage and prepare her for the tribulation, we poured a bumper of rum which, after she had taken the first gulp, made the round among us all. It made us wilder than ever.

"Changing places, the two strange men simultaneously fucked me as Bertie and Topsy had done while the latter were lashing away at the victim until she begged for mercy.

"That orgiastic scene in which one fucked, masturbated, sucked, bawled and yelled became indescribable.

"When the uproar was at its height, a detachment of police broke in and arrested us all. The two men, who were absolutely drunk, were led to the calaboose, but we women were able to get off.

"That outcome covered me with shame and confusion. I hastily dressed as best I could. The sergeant, recognising that I was of a different class from the two other girls, offered to take me back home. When I told him who I was and how I happened to find myself in such a predicament, he was understanding, warned me not to let it happen again, and helped me as much as he could.

"Leading me through the obscure lanes and holding me by the arm, he noticed that I had difficulty in walking. My legs were barely able to support me. He asked if I wished to rest a moment. Since we were barely halfway home, I gratefully agreed to his suggestion. I was truly exhausted.

" 'There's just the spot for a pause,' he suddenly cried.

"Pushing aside a gate, he led me into a sort of courtyard where there were several small hay-ricks. He seated me on one of them and then took his place at my side, holding me by the waist.

" 'You have no idea, Mademoiselle, how sorry I felt for you,' he sympathised. 'There is no doubt that you were tricked into such a house of ill-fame. But I am more than happy at having been able to offer you my services, such as they are. But, truly, don't you think I deserve a little compensation.?'

" 'To be sure, Sergeant,' I replied. 'What can I do to show my gratitude?'

" 'Hee, hee!' he tittered. 'Take me in your arms and permit me to kiss your seductive lips. If you allow me that, I shall feel more than amply rewarded.'

" 'It certainly would be impolite of me to refuse, but I know that I can count on your discretion. Kiss me if that is what your heart dictates. Oh! But

I did not give you permission to put your hand there. That was not included in your request.'

" 'That's true,' he admitted. 'But the glimpse I had of your hidden beauties has so excited me that you could not, would not, I am sure, refuse me permission to make more intimate acquaintance-ship with them.'

"Without any trace of embarrassment, he had placed his hand squarely on my mound and with his fingers began to touch and explore the surround-ings. Then throwing me back on the rick, he spread open my thighs with his knees while he opened his trousers and drew out his prick which he put in my hand.

"The night was dark and I could not see this new instrument of pleasure, but it felt uncommonly large and powerful. Its head seemed to be shaking with suppressed energy.

"In the course of the evening, I had been fucked nine times by four different pricks. And now at the contact of the fifth, which would have won the prize had there been a contest, I felt my desires being refired more ardently than ever.

" 'Well, what do you think of Jack. (Jack was the name he gave to his organ)?' he demanded. 'Don't you think it is capable of giving you as much enjoy-ment as any of those to which you granted your favours?'

"Saying that, he brutally shoved 'Jack' between my lips. I gingerly took the head into my mouth, but it was so huge that I could barely fit it in.

" 'How good that feels,' he moaned. 'Now, my dear girl, spread your legs.'

"No sooner had I done so than I felt the monster in my cunt.

" 'Don't you feel Jack plunging into you?' he cried ecstatically.

"Indeed, I did. Although my legs were as far apart as I could stretch them, his organ was crammed into my hollow to the utmost.

"The sergeant was an old experienced fucker. He fucked me with such decision and verve that each thrust struck a responsive chord in my heart. He was the one who possessed me after the others had merely roused me, and it was he who really gave me true gratification. When it was over, I was so worn out and exhausted that I could not rise to my feet. He had to carry me the rest of the way home.

"The next morning, the obliging sergeant came to discreetly ask news of me. He took advantage of our conversation to tell me that the affair was turning out badly. There certainly was going to be an inquiry, he continued, and he advised me that if I did not wish to appear as a witness, I should leave the city as quickly as possible.

"Just about that time, my uncle had asked me to go and spend some time with his ailing wife. You can be sure that I leaped at the chance. Hastening my departure, I was thus able to escape the scandal.

"In the meantime, my father and my aunt died, after which I became the ward of my uncle. That explains my presence on board the *Camarilla*."

"You certainly have the ability to tell a story," I exclaimed. "And with so much imagination. My poor pussy is on fire. Won't you be good enough to put your hand on it and with your fingers try to extinguish the blaze that is consuming it? While you are making love, you'll tell me how you were able to conceal from your uncle the loss of your virginity and how it came about that you accorded him your favours."

"Anything you say, my dear," Laura replied. "Lift up your legs so I can have a better look at your clitoris which I am going to stimulate. In turn, you'll render me the same service while I continue my recital. Push down hard, my love.

"Since you are already aware of the Captain's amative disposition, you'll easily understand that while I was taking care of his wife, he renewed his efforts to persuade me to do what he had in mind. While I was starving for a prick and a good fuck, I felt some aversion for him, primarily because he was my mother's brother. Therefore, I did my best to avoid being alone with him, and every night before going to bed, I carefully locked the door to my room.

"In the end, he succeeded in persuading me to join him on a boat ride that he was planning. Our goal was a little island about a dozen miles out to sea and famed for its beauty.

"When we left, the weather was superb and the sea was as smooth as glass. Suddenly a violent storm threatened and the Captain decided that we should go back. As the weather became more stormy, we headed for the nearest port. It was late when we reached shore, and the spot where we landed was opposite from the one we had left.

"I was half dead with fear, agonisingly seasick, and soaked to the marrow. Looking up at the heavens, he immediately renounced any idea of returning to the home port. Instead, he took me to a little hotel, whose proprietor was one of his friends.

"At supper, he did his best to cheer me up, but

I was really ill and had to go to bed. There had been prepared for me a little room which led from the living-room. As soon as I was alone in it, I happily took off my damp clothing and slid under the cool sheets.

"After his dinner, my uncle ordered coffee which he brought into my room. When he tried to make me drink some, he found that I was shaking with fever.

" 'Oh, my poor girl,' he commiserated. 'How your teeth are chattering. You must have caught a terrible cold. I'll have to get you something to warm you up and restore the circulation of your blood.'

"He went out, prepared a heavily spiced grog, and came back to my side. Avidly, I gulped down the hot brew for I was chilled through and through. But it was stronger than I thought, and it went to my head.

"I was seated up in my bed and my uncle had his arm tenderly enwrapped around my waist. He seemed very exhilarated.

"Turning toward him, I said with a nervous laugh: "Uncle, I feel so dizzy. What should I do?'

" 'Nothing for the moment,' he replied. 'Just rest easy with your head on my chest, and the giddiness will soon disappear.'

"As I allowed myself to relax, he squeezed me more tightly and began to caress my budding breasts. I was too weak to put up any resistance. Soon I felt his hand under my nightgown and on my pussy. I clutched it before it could go any farther.

" 'Oh, Uncle, how could you ever dare try something like that? Aren't you forgetting that I am your niece? That is not right what you are doing. Take away your hand.'

" 'There is no reason for you to protest, Laura. I am old enough to be your father and my standing as your uncle gives me the right to teach you all over. Come, release my hand. I just want to rub you on this spot. It will do you a world of good. Don't make any fuss now.'

"He succeeded in getting his hand down to my cunt, into whose crevice he inserted two fingers between my lips.

" 'Uncle, uncle! I'm starting to feel sick. Let me down.'

"He allowed me to recline without, however, taking away his hand from between my thighs.

" 'Oh, my darling,' he sighed as he kissed me. 'My dearly beloved Laura, I adore you as I have never before adored anyone. As you know, your aunt is dying, and I shall never re-marry. It is my intention to adopt you, for I already look on you as my daughter. And if you consent to give me the proof of your love that I so desire, all my fortune will be yours one day.'

"As he was delivering his little speech, he did not cease stimulating my lower regions.

"Soon I felt myself penetrated by a salutary warmth. My blood was flowing more freely and arousing my organs. No longer making any attempt to defend myself, I allowed him to spread my legs and, after he had removed the covers, to put his mouth to my pussy.

"More and more I became fidgety. My hand which was brushing his was trembling as if in quest of some object it could not find. Aware of what I was doing, he took my groping hand with a smile and placed it on his member.

"Immediately, I had my fingers around it and

117

gently rubbed up and down its soft skin while amorously caressing the satiny head.

"The route to bliss opened wide. My uncle quickly divested himself of his clothing. Then, taking firm hold of me, he positioned me across the bed with my buttocks facing the ceiling. After regarding with obvious pleasure for several moments the rosy slit that met his eyes, he embraced me in a passionate hug. Then he commenced that delicious motion which, although as old as Eve, remains eternally young and always delights her daughters who possess health and heart.

"What more can I tell you. Regine? He took his enjoyment of me to his heart's content, only leaving me to regain my forces in restoring sleep.

"When I awoke the next morning, I found myself in his arms. His wonderful gland, the power of which I had experienced the night before, was again rigid and aimed at its favourite target. With transports, I seized it while the Captain, tossing off the sheets and blanket, despoiled me of my nightgown and gave himself up to a thorough and minute exploration of my entire body.

"As most men do, he went into ecstasies over my cunt, praising it to the high heavens. Then he asked me to lie on him, with my pussy on his mouth, and to suck him. Without a moment's hesitation, I obeyed, placing my backside on his face so that we were head to foot. While his organ was swimming in my mouth, I had his testicles in my hand. They soon began to swell which, with a man, indicates ejaculation. I was not mistaken. A few seconds later, a hot jet of sperm gushed into my mouth, and drop by drop, it descended down to the bottom

118

of my throat. The liquid was as intoxicating as champagne.

"Such were the beginnings of the intimacy with my uncle Saint-Jean. I am his niece, but, to a certain extent, I am also his mistress.

"To tell the truth, the liaison has been advantageous and delightful for me, but it is not one of those that should be stretched out too long. I have made up my mind to put an end to it without hurting his feelings if that is possible. Your presence here and my forthcoming marriage with Lieutenant Yeats will give me the opportunity, I hope, that I am looking for. Well, time will tell."

BOOK III

CHAPTER IX

THE HONEYMOON

When we arrived at Port-Royal, we heard that civil war had just broken out in America. There Captain Saint-Jean found some letters from his shipping company.

They were orders for him to set sail for Trinidad with Sir Charles Stanhope, the new governor there, as a passenger. The Captain was also instructed to make the necessary arrangements on board for not only the lord, but also for his family consisting of the Honourable Lady Stanhope, their daughter, and their servants. There were certain delays. The Governor requested several days in order to complete preparations for his transfer.

Captain Saint-Jean decided to take advantage of the sailing postponement to celebrate Laura's nuptials prior to the departure.

We all took quarters in the city where Laura and Mr. William Yeats were duly united in bonds of matrimony. The Captain and I served as witnesses.

Our little group was augmented by an old friend of the Captain. His name was Johnny, and he was accompanied by a pretty young mulatto woman who was full of life and gaiety. She was called Betsy, and that is all I knew about her.

After a sumptuous wedding lunch washed down

with vintage champagne, we clambered into our carriage which was to bear us to a rustic inn nearby where rooms had been reserved for us for the night.

Billy and his young bride were lifted into a cabriolet, and as they sped off with their eyes modestly lowered, we followed them for a time, bombarding them with old shoes and rice and wishing them a happy and above all a fertile marriage.

As for ourselves, we set off in a sort of a charabanc with the word "buggy" written all over its sides. A handsome Negro was our driver.

I found myself seated next to our new comrade Johnny. The Captain was facing me alongside of Betsy whose waist he was embracing with his arm. His jovial face was almost glued to the fresh cheeks of his new conquest.

We really were a merry band. The occasion and the atmosphere, all charged that day with the rustle of spring, and the champagne which we had copiously consumed, contributed to inflame our senses and arouse our lewd desires.

We began to bicker about where and how to rest our legs. To the contrary of what is usually done, the Captain insisted that each man must put his between those of his female adversary. Betsy and I protested, but Johnny declared that for the time being, the vehicle was the same as the Captain's ship, and since he had absolute command while on board, we had to acquiesce in his decision.

During the ensuing little scuffle, it was discovered that Betsy was wearing blue garters. Johnny lauded their beauty and elegance but wagered that mine must be at least equally attractive. I was summoned to put mine on view to the group.

The captain heartily seconded the motion, and,

holding my legs firmly, he managed to flip up my skirts to the great amusement of the coachman who was looking at us over his shoulder. He was smiling from ear to ear.

Betsy, who had joyfully joined in the game, suddenly cried: "Regine's garters are scarlet, that I can see, but I know that she has something a little higher up that is of a much lovelier colour and well deserving of your inspection."

"Speak for yourself, Mademoiselle Patent Leather," I retorted. "And what shade is yours at that spot?"

"Go to it!" shouted the Captain as he shoved his knees under my thighs, tumbling me backwards, while Johnny managed to settle himself between my legs. "Don't back down! Go ahead! Johnny, turn the key in the hole.'

"Ha, ha!" Betsy, delighted by my embarrassment, guffawed. "Ha, it is very well to talk about the key, but where is the key? I don't see a sign of one."

"You won't say that any more, Betsy," the Captain interrupted. "Here's one key at least!" With that he waved one in full state of erection under her nose. "I'm sure that Johnny is not going to fail you and me by not producing a key."

"Attention, everybody!" Johnny burst out. "Here's another."

He promptly unbuttoned his fly from which popped out a magnificent prick at least nine inches long, hard as steel, and topped by a purple crown.

"What did I tell you?" exclaimed the Captain. "It's all yours, Regine. Grab it before it gets away from you. You're in luck, Johnny. Isn't she a choice morsel?"

Betsy, to the Captain's great joy, could not keep her eyes from his "key". She opened still wider his trousers from which she extracted an admirable pair of testicles. While one of her hands lasciviously tickled his rear opening, the other began to stroke, delicately and expertly, the gland that was wriggling and vibrating with pleasure.

As you can well imagine, my new friend's hands were not idle. One of them was lovingly smacking her rounded bottom, and the other was tickling her cunt that was just beginning to open its flaps.

Johnny and I were not slow in following their example, and we soon were playing a quartette. His titillations on my pussy threw me into such a pitch of excitement that I readily agreed, nay, with enthusiasm, to his suggestion that I sit with my bare backside on his knees and allow his stunning organ to make its way through the lips of my source of delight.

Luckily for us, there was little or no traffic on the road we were taking. As a result, we were able to violate every known rule of decency. Just as there is a god who watches over drunks, there is another for fuckers. Once in a while we passed some slaves, but they scarcely gave us a glance. We were in perfect safety.

I perched on Johnny who was voluptuously rubbing my buttocks with the thick bush covering his belly. Then I lifted my skirts still higher so that the Captain and Betsy would not miss a detail of our activity. I widened my groove and into it soon disappeared to the hilt the beloved dirk.

"Bravo, bravo!" shouted the Captain. "As usual, Regine has struck the first blow. Let us follow her example of courage!" he continued, ordering Betsy to lift up her poop-deck and plug her slit with his cork.

Obviously accustomed to games of this sort, Betsy did not have to be persuaded. Lewdly baring her generous posterior, she rested her plump hemispheres on the Captain's lap, while the latter with a quick and deft hand fastened the head of his prick to the entrance of the vagina. Hastily lowering her rump, she roared with a burst of laughter:

"Ah, now I've got the key. My, how it jiggles trying to get in my keyhole!"

Both of us females, thus solidly pegged from behind, began to move convulsively on our seats. Bending forward, we embraced each other and rested our heads on the other's shoulder. Johnny took advantage of the fact that Betsy's face was within his reach, enabling him to exchange tongues with her while his generous virility was valiantly poking in my fane of delights.

"Oh," exclaimed Betsy, turning her head around for a moment, "what fun this is. We are really a quartet of love. Inside of me I feel the Captain's rod pumping up and down while his lecherous fingers are bringing disgrace to my rose-leaf. As for myself, I am fingering the luscious lips of Regine whose cunt is aromatic with Johnny's perfume. And, my God, Johnny is forcing his gland into my mouth. Oof! I'm going out of my mind it is so divine!" With a sonorous voice, she burst into the well-known sailors' song:

Come, my dears, let's fuck with ardour,
Let the rumps and cunts, the pricks
    and the tongues

127

Serve us as oars to advance forward
On the sea of delight, the vessel of love.

This maritime ditty amused us no end and we
nearly split our sides from laughter as the jolts of
the carriage on the bumpy road jostled and threw
us back and forth.

As you can easily imagine, the men had promptly
discharged, but they found their positions so agreeable that they begged us to let them remain as they
were.

Our ebony chauffeur took an infinite pleasure in
our games. Turning around to look at us, he showed
us an enormous grin and dazzling white teeth. Now
he was dividing his attention between us and his
driving with his head turning back and forth like a
puppet manipulated by a string. Finally, the good
fellow could hold himself back no longer. He was
so convulsed with laughter that we thought he was
going to fall off his perch. While he was in those
spasms, a black tool escaped from his pants which
did not seem to have any buttons.

"Get going, Pompey," shouted the Captain. "A
half-turn to the right, my boy, so that these ladies
can admire that wonderful bald-headed bird that
you keep caged there."

Pompey obeyed.

"Good ladies and gentlemen, I am just a poor
black with too much meat for little holes like the
ladies'!"

Without any warning, he threw between Betsy
and myself the florid head of his unbelievable prick.
Betsy immediately caught it, since she was the
closest, and she generously put it to my mouth.

I have to confess that I have always had a weakness for black pricks. I immediately took possession of it, inserting the tip between my lips while I massaged the satiny skin of the muscular column.

The sight of Pompey's majestic organ stuck deep in my mouth exhilarated my companions and urged them on to greater efforts.

Saint-Jean's face was beaming with pleasure while Betsy's buttocks, rising and falling like the tides of the sea, took his organ between the orbs and introduced it into her slit. With each thrust, she screamed: "Oh, Captain, my Captain, fuck me. Fuck me once again!"

As if I were drunk, I wiggled my bottom back and forth on Johnny's thighs. Then, just at the moment I felt his tumescent appendage flood my lower regions, an abundant gush of sticky fluid spouted into my mouth from the noble and vigorous fountain of Pompey. I savoured each drop of it. While my hands pressured his swollen testicles as if to drain them dry, my lips enclosed the copious engine which kept pumping down my throat the invigorating liquid.

I took in this ejaculation with an enjoyment far superior to what I was accustomed to.

It would take me too long to tell you everything that went on in our cart, now transformed into one of Venus's chariots. The entire ride was nothing but an uninterrupted orgy of lewdness and lubricity.

With the greatest amiability, the Captain greeted the women we met on the way. They seemed to understand him perfectly. Often they replied to his pleasantries with a nod or a broad smile of their sensuous lips.

"How's your little pussy, Sarah?" he cried out.

"Not too bad, Massah, thank you. The only thing wrong is that it doesn't have a tail.

"Well, here's one for you. At your service, Sarah. Take a close look at it. Would you like it for your kitten?"

"Many thanks, Massah. It's really a fine one. But your pretty friend's cat will miss it."

They left, laughing heartily.

When the ride was finally over, we learned that Billy and his bride were locked in their room. After having listened a moment to the joyous squeaks of the bed-springs, the Captain put his mouth to the keyhole and gaily cried out:

"Hello, Lieutenant. How's your health, Laura?"

"Oh, Uncle I am nearly dead. Billy is killing me with his . . . "

"Don't listen to a word she says, Saint-Jean.

Right now, her rump is covering my face with her backside and she is draining my reservoir dry and covering herself with my life's blood."

"Ha, ha. All the better. But don't overdo it, my friends, or, if you have to commit suicide, do so promptly, for we are dying of hunger."

We were soon seated around a sumptuously served table. Since the waiters kept hovering around us, we maintained appearances, merely exchanging suggestive leers and playing footsie under the table.

The owner of the hotel, a Mr Toots, a very distinguished looking quadroon, appeared very happy to have us as guests, for there was always a smile on his lips when he addressed us.

The idea came to me that Pompey probably betrayed some of our secrets to him. Indeed, all evening, he never stopped regarding us from the corner of his eye. From his expression, I gathered that he was determined to join in our games by hook or crook.

His pretty wife seemed to have the same intentions, for each time that she came to replenish our glasses, she devoured the Captain and Johnny with her eyes.

Because of the smallness of the inn, we were only able to obtain three rooms and a salon. It was decided that Betsy and I would share one, Johnny and the Captain the second, and the newlyweds the third.

After a healthy nightcap of grog, we retired to our respective chambers. Betsy and I noticed that ours was between Laura's and the owners. Since the partitions were paper thin, we heard on both sides, to the right and to the left, a number of amusing sounds and suggestive whispers that made us giggle. But I was so tired and so influenced by the alcohol that I could not keep my eyes open. The last thing I remembered was Betsy fumbling between my thighs.

I had been asleep for several hours when I was awakened by my bed partner's hand which seemed to be caressing my cunt. Having thrown off my covers, she was now busily exploring the insides of my thighs.

"Oh, Betsy, no, I beg of you," I pleaded as I made a motion to push away her fingers. But she seized my hand and held it tightly.

"What a big, powerful hand you have, Betsy!" I whispered. "And what is that you're pushing between the lips of my pussy? Is it a dildo? Where in the devil did you get it? Oh, put it in right away.

How big and well-shaped it is. I would swear that it is a genuine prick that is fucking me."

At the same instant, I heard a big laugh which was not at all feminine. Shoving aside the hand that I had been holding, I felt an outrageously hairy male and a magisterial organ which was splitting my cunt wide open.

"Who are you?" I squealed, straightening up and trying to put my hand to the face of the man who was fucking me incognito.

In a twinkling, a torrent of sperm was inundating my love receptacle. The result of his hot overflow was to put an end to my protests. I was overwhelmed with caresses from the unknown who was lying in a semi-faint across my breast.

Then I realised—as undoubtedly many have realised before me and many will realise after me—that once a woman's cunt is satisfied, once she has said her last word, she has manifested her sole reason for being and that henceforth she becomes for a time a simple machine in the hands of her conqueror.

Although the discharge was copious, the gland remained immersed in my hollow without losing an inch of its length. Our tongues enlaced and became welded into one.

The man did not remain inactive for long. Aroused by the internal contractions of my vagina which furiously was acting like a nutcracker, he passed his hands under my derriere, raised my buttocks, and began again his superb performance.

Determined not to let pass by such a wonderful opportunity, I spread wide my legs and humped up my cunt while my fingernails feverishly scratched his firm buttocks.

Alas, only three times. How tenuous earthly joys are! And of such short duration. At the very moment when our ardent desires were about to blend in one supreme moment of bliss, an apparition came to cut us short and paralyse us with fear.

A tall skinny woman in a sweeping white dressing-gown and a nightcap on her almost bald head suddenly appeared behind my valiant horseman.

"Ah, Toots, you scoundrel, you rogue. So here I find you, you vile wretch. So your legally wedded spouse is insufficient for you. You debauched rake! You old lecher! It is not enough that you fuck the servants, but you have to insult your honourable women who are our guests. Get that out of her, you satyr, or I'll . . . !" she screamed in a piercing voice. Putting down the lamp she was carrying on the table, she launched herself on her husband, grabbed him by the haunches, and tried to separate him from me.

Deaf to her screeches, he clung to me like a drowning man. Everything seemed to be happening, the earth opening up and the sky falling down. In spite of all that or perhaps because of it, he was determined to finish the job.

Nevertheless, the frightful racket caused by a woman in fury did not fail to have some effect. A door opened and other actors appeared on the stage. The Captain and Johnny followed by a dishevelled Betsy, all three bearing candles, erupted into my room.

"Forward! Forward!" the Captain cried. "Don't lose heart, my friends. Two against one. The odds are in our favour."

Lunging on Madame Toots, he dragged her back

so violently that both tumbled backwards on the floor.

During the struggle, the good lady's dressing-gown had come open from top to bottom and the jubilant Captain found himself a prisoner between her legs. The result of this position, as suggestive as unexpected, was not long in coming. Before you could say "Jack Robinson," the inflated gland dove headfirst into the lady's hollow.

"Toots! . . . Toots! . . . You brigand . . . You blackguard . . . Coward . . . Are you going to remain there like a milksop and let your wife be raped under your very eyes?"

Toots merely turned his head to her and winked. "Take it in good part, Mama," he said placidly, and as if nothing had happened, he immediately went back to his task which had been so rudely interrupted.

"Ah, Regine, how did this all come about? But don't worry about it. You won't have reason to complain," he assured me.

I felt his fingers touching his big organ, which, happily, was able to continue its job in my cunt on the verge of the supreme enjoyment.

Johnny, who had paused in amazement at the spectacle, believed it was high time that he took an active role in it. Noticing the particularly favourable posture Betsy had assumed with her rear in the air, he hurried to flip up her nightgown and expose two magnificent ebony hemispheres adorably dimpled. Then, with a sure hand, he guided his rigid masculinity through the russet thicket and plunged it as far as he could into the humid redoubt that was burning with desire.

As was his wont, the Captain was overjoyed with

a new cunt, even though it was as broken from usage as that of his wife. Moreover, Saint-Jean felt himself pricked with new yearning on seeing Johnny in action with Betsy and with renewed ardour, he redoubled his efforts.

Our three vessels were being adored as they never had been before. In their turn, the three virilities found themselves deliciously engaged in their favourite sport. So everything had turned out for the best, and nobody had cause for complaint.

When Madame Toots saw that Betsy and I were obviously not experiencing any repugnance to the gay party, she let down what hair she had and whole-heartedly joined in the fun.

She was unable to contain herself and proved to be insatiable. She kept wanting more and more. It was only after she had been more than copiously fucked by each of the three men that she declared that she finally had enough.

Before taking his leave, old Mr Toots confided in us that the hag had never given him so much enjoyment as that evening.

We rested for several hours, and it was high time, and after a nourishing and restoring breakfast, we all returned to Port-Royal. Thus ended my friend Laura's honeymoon.

CHAPTER X

THE GOVERNOR AND HIS FAMILY

Knowing that he would have to return to Jamaica within a few weeks, the Captain generously told Yeats to take leave on shore in order that he could take a short holiday with his new wife. He should have no worry for he and the second mate could divide up his duties. Before sailing, he gave his son-in-law very discreetly the handsome dowry he had promised his niece.

So that I will not have to refer to the matter any more, I shall finish up with what I knew about Laura and her husband.

Both were very grateful to Captain Saint-Jean. At their home, his room was always ready and when he got the idea of calling on them, he was always given a warm welcome. But when he tried to obtain from Laura the execution of the agreed contract, she declared that she had no intention of keeping it, even though she was fully aware of the goodness he had shown her and her spouse. Also, Billy was of the same mind.

She was so madly in love with him and he acquitted himself so admirably in his marital duties that she had no wish to know any other man.

At first, the Captain seemed chagrined by the rebuff, gently put as it was, but gradually, his basic good nature won over his lower desires. Never again did he broach the subject to his niece whom he really loved and respected. Henceforth, a peck on the cheek was enough to satisfy him, and he willingly assumed the role of an affectionate father.

This leads me to express a thought which I have often pondered. What a pity it is to see how few husbands and wives have the courage to renounce voluntarily stupid and irritating jealousy! I am positive that if they enjoyed each other's confidence, there would be fewer conjugal infidelities.

By nature, we women, if we feel that we are spied on and held captive, are aroused to more intense and profound yearnings for liberty. This freedom that we so desire, let it be ours, and if we have it, we shall renounce it of our free will.

But let us get back to our story. Finally, we could get under way for Jamaica with the Governor and his suite aboard. Sir Charles, a man of ripe age, was the personification of the elderly English gentleman, with manners that were courteous and affable. From the first day out, he showered me with his attentions.

That seemed to arouse the anger of his wife, who was a jealous prude. She made no attempt to hide her cool feelings toward me, and soon as she spotted her husband and myself in a conversation, she swooped down on us like a bird of prey. With bitter reproaches, she accused her spouse of neglecting her, and if looks could kill, I would have been long since dead. And I was so innocent of any wrongdoing.

"Very well, Milady," I said to myself, "who

strews wind reaps a tempest. Since you will have brought it on yourself, so much the worse for you. I am going to let matters take their course, and you will have only yourself to blame for whatever happens."

The Captain had turned over his cabin to the Governor while he used his son-in-law's. Sir Charles' daughter, Miss Blanche, had been assigned to the stateroom next to mine. It had formerly been occupied by Laura.

Miss Blanche Stanhope was a bit older than I. Snobbish about her noble birth and her father's exalted position, she was cold and formal. She affected an air of modesty, nay, prudery, but her eyes bespoke the contrary. I promised myself to keep a watch over her to determine if my hunch was correct.

She had an English personal maid, who was so seasick that she required more attention than her mistress.

As his valet, the Governor had an Italian named Sporio who seemed to labour under the impresssion that his prime duty was to occupy himself with the women, particularly the youngest ones.

The Captain often found himself torn between them in their arguments, and I bet that he wished he had Billy with him to smooth over the squabbles.

He and I had many hearty laughs by ourselves at their foibles. We dubbed Lady Stanhope "drop at the end of the nose" from her habit of taking snuff. Miss Blanche had been baptised "flamingo" because of her haughtiness and the bright scarlet dress that she customarily wore on deck.

At the beginning, they all suffered in varying degree from the inevitable seasickness. The first to recover was the Governor who believed it was a good time to worm himself into my good graces. Because of his wife's discourteous behaviour, I received his advances with more frigidity than I otherwise would have.

Delighted at the chance to put one over on the old woman, the Captain took the Governor's side and attempted to help him in his enterprise as best he could.

That day after the sun had set, we spent a charming evening chatting in our deck-chairs on the stern of the ship. Because she was still ailing, Milady was unable to favour us with her amiable and gracious presence. As for Miss Blanche, the fear of having her fresh complexion chapped by the sea breezes forced her to regain the salon.

The nice old Governor revealed himself to be something of a gay dog. When he and I were alone, he wrapped me in a blanket to protect me from the dampness. Then, after a few squeezes of the hand and a gallant discourse, he ventured to favour me with a kiss.

Encouraged by my failure to protest, he bent more deeply over me and enlaced me in his arms.

"My dear Regine," he declared, "you are one of the most attractive, adorable young women I have ever met. Every time that I find myself at your side, I experience an ineffable joy. If only I could have all of you, even if it were for a minute, I believe I could die happy."

"Nonsense, Milord," I laughed. "I wager that you tell that to every pretty girl you meet. But, Sir Charles, what would your wife say if she saw us so close to each other?"

"Don't bother your pretty little head about that

139

old witch. She is in no state to bother us. Please let me, my dear. I would love you so much more. And I shall give you anything that your heart desires."

Turning me around, he tried to slip his hand up under my skirt.

"Oh, Sir Charles, that is very naughty. I never would have thought it of you. It is true that I am very fond of you, but I could never permit anything like that."

But the old lecher had too much experience with women to be put off by such a feeble argument. After some effort, he succeeded in introducing his hand between my thighs. Pushing me to the rear, he bent over me and held me on my back while his fingers wandered over my *mons veneris*.

"Oh, Sir Charles, take away your hand. You're no gentleman," I squealed.

"What firm and shapely legs you have, my dear. And this mossy little niche, how warm and silky it is! What a delightful morsel you are. Spread your thighs, darling, and allow me to get between them. That's fine. Now don't be afraid. I want to make love to you without any distractions."

"I beg you," I pleaded with mock anguish. "Please stop. No, I am really afraid someone may come. How can you dare, right here on the deck?"

I sensed that he was stealthily opening the front of his trousers to release his prisoner.

"Woe is me. Heavens! What are you going to do? No, no, don't you dare stick that in me. I am lost. Sir Charles! You are so clumsy. Oh, no, it is in. Be careful, milord. Take it easy at first. I do hope that the Captain won't surprise us."

After some difficulties, he had managed to get his prick into me. I found it neither particularly big nor vigorous, and to facilitate his task, I spread a little wider and pressed him tenderly to my breast.

"Oh, my dear, what a delicious little grotto you have. It fits me like a glove. Shove up a little so that I can get deeper into you. Do cooperate with me. Ah, this is something I haven't had in over twenty years. Does it feel good? Tell me, does my poor little instrument give you any enjoyment?"

I lied a little to give him encouragement.

"Oh, indeed yes, Sir Charles. I'm in seventh heaven. But in the name of God, do be careful. Don't go too far and don't stay too long inside. Suppose I would get pregnant. Oh, I'm afraid, so take care."

After several more thrusts and with a quivering sigh, he ejaculated his liquid.

"You poor thing,' he murmured from a half-faint as he rested on my breast, "did I hurt you? Do you know, it was so hard for me to get it into you?"

"Yes, Sir Charles," I agreed. "At first, you caused me very much pain, but once your beloved instrument was all the way to the bottom, I experienced the sweetest delights."

"How innocent you are, my treasure. (Little did he know.) I am going to teach you all the joys of love. Would you like me to fuck you again? Say the word 'fuck.' "

"Fuck," I repeated in my most girlish tone. 'Fuck. Yes, Sir Charles, you can fuck me again if you like, Sir Charles."

"Say—'With my prick in your cunt,' " he insisted.

"If that gives any pleasure. (Innocently.) With your prick in my cunt. Is that right?"

"Perfect," he replied enthusiastically. "Let me

141

kiss you for your kindness. Now, permit me to put my hands under your adorable little derriere so that I can fondle those two smooth thighs. With your fingers, keep squeezing my prick while I sweep it across your cunt."

I clutched his aged organ. Although it was flaccid and dry, it seemed still able to function a little. In order to excite him, I began to play with his sagging testicles.

The old fogey seemed to enjoy that thoroughly. A bit of his youth returned and he fucked me as well as he could.

"Thank you, thank you a thousand times, dearest Regine," he exclaimed gratefully. "You have warmed my ageing blood. For a moment, I thought I was thirty years younger."

While what I have just recounted went on, the Captain had come and seen what we were up to. Discreetly he withdrew and kept away anyone who might have disturbed us.

During the following days, we attempted to renew the little celebration, but it was impossible—we were unable to escape the inquisitorial eyes of mother and daughter. Nevertheless shortly afterwards, I learned something about Miss Blanche and her doings which redressed the balance between us.

My chambermaid Zilla, whom the reader may remember since I spoke of her in some of the preceding chapters, kept me informed as to what she was up to. She told me all about the flirtation and how, without any hesitation, she had given herself to the quartermaster and the ship's carpenter, letting each believe that it was the first time for her, that each was the first to enjoy her favours

This piquant situation could have continued for a long time had not, one fine night, the two come for her precisely at the same moment and at the same spot. The show was given away, but as sensible men, they decided not to quarrel but enjoy her in common. It was, assuredly, the wisest course, and it resulted in an enhancement of their pleasures. They could fuck her by taking turns or by having her simultaneously. Zilla was of the opinion that the last was the best.

The most recent conquest of my soubrette was Sporio, the Governor's valet.

She told me that he was absolutely wild about her and that his pet name for her was "my adored Negress." Also, she mentioned that she scolded him for the devotion he showed to Miss Blanche, to which he replied that the English girl was nothing in his eyes compared to her. If Zilla wanted him to do so, he was ready to give Miss Blanche her walking papers.

So virginal in the eyes of the world, Miss Blanche nursed a passion for him. She even succeeded in obtaining permission from her father to let Sporio give her Italian lessons in her stateroom, for the roll of the ship was more pronounced in the salon and it unsettled her. He did not like to be alone with her, he said, for all she did was stroke and suck his prick.

When I told Captain Saint-Jean the state of affairs, he was seized by a fit of wild laughter which distorted his mouth and nearly broke his ribs.

"Ho, ho, ho! I can't get over it. Just think of the snooty flamingo pumping that little beggar. That would be something to see. I would give anything. Regine, I have made up my mind. We are going to spy on them. The partitions that separate these two staterooms are removable. Get back on deck and stay there. As long as those two women can see you, they won't budge an inch. That will give me a free hand and time to do what I have in mind."

A little later, he came to get me. There was a gleam of malicious joy in his eyes.

"Everything is ready," he chuckled, rubbing his hands. "You can stand sentry duty as of now. Keep your eyes open, but be cautious. Once you are in your cabin, carefully pull towards you the false moulding on the partition to the left of your bunk. You'll feel the panel move. Push it to the right until you come to a peephole wide enough for you to see into the flamingo's nest. I wager you'll witness something piquant quite soon. But don't miss a detail, for I expect a complete report. Hurry up, now. I barely had got rid of my equipment when she started coming down. Also, I heard her tell Sporio to go and bring her some tea and not to forget his Italian dictionary."

I needed no further urging. As I crossed the salon, I ascertained that Miss Blanche's door was shut. In my stateroom, I latched the the door behind me and drew the curtain over the port hole. Following the Captain's instruction, I drew the panel until I came to the aperture he mentioned.

The tableau offered to my view was both astonishing and charming. It was better than I had dared hope for. Stretched out on a divan, Sporio was reading in a low voice some passages from a book in his hand.

His trousers were wide open in the front, while Blanche was seated next to him on a footstool. Her head was leaning on him as she was clutching wit

144

both her hands his olive-coloured prick. She was kissing it while her fingers agilely ran up and down the column.

It was a good-sized member streaked with blue veins. The head was haughtily erect as if it were conscious of being the adored plaything which a rather frigid woman would love to cajole and ensconce in her pocket of love.

The book that Sporio was reading from was the *Decameron* in the original Italian. Blanche was repeating after him, sentence by sentence, and often interrupting him to ask a question.

They were on the tenth story of the third day, the one concerning the innocent Alibech asking the hermit Rusticus how one accomplishes the pious task of "shoving the Devil back into hell." One recalls that the silly thing thought that the robust organ of the holy man, the sight of which struck her dumb with astonishment, was Satan come to conquer and martyrise him:

" 'How happy I am,' she cried, 'at not having a devil there to torment me as it must you.'

" 'But, Alibech, you have on the same spot the blazing inferno where we have to return him.'

"With libertine fingers, the recluse caresses the sanctuary which, up until then, had never been violated. "Permit me, my dear child, to insert this diabolic creature into this hell. If we do so, we shall both experience celestial delights.' "

"Innocently and devoutly, the child allows the man of God to perform the meritorious act as she with an unconscious lasciviousness bends every effort to assist him.

"The hermit places her in the position most favourable to his evil designs. Partially opening the

145

shaded gates of her amorous convent, he begins to cram the devil into it.

" 'Oh, father, what a wicked devil it is! He is hurting me so much. I am suffering as much as if I, too, were in Hell."

"It is not long, however, before she finds so delicious the prolonged vibrations of the devil in his hell that she begs him not to stop his pious labours.

"She turned out to be so greedy, accusing him of laziness and slothfulness, that, after several more assaults, he retired, exhausted and worn out, from the insatiable inferno."

Miss Blanche seemed to be very amused at Alibech's unconscious voluptuousness.

"But, after all, I don't blame her in the slightest if Brother Rusticus had as handsome a devil as you have there and who seems to be desirous of plunge into the amorous pool awaiting him."

She fondled it again.

"Why, look," she exclaimed in surprise. "It's weeping just at the thought of it."

With a lick of her tongue, she skimmed off the milky drop glistening on the head.

"You're right, carissima. It is weeping. How do you want me to put it into you today?"

"Stretch out all the way on the divan and I'll get on top of you. I'll introduce it in myself. You'll see for yourself if I can handle the Devil or not."

Lifting up her skirts, she tucked them in around her waist. Then, leaping on to the sofa, she bestrode the Italian.

With a flip, she raised his shirt, bent over the purple-headed demon, clutched it, and following it with a lubricious glance, directed it towards the wooded entrance of the cavern. When she felt it warmly nestled inside, she gave a jerk backwards, and now, with a solid support on her knees, she lent herself to the cadence of the ship's roll. Shortly her thighs were lasciviously quivering.

From her movements, it was easy to see that she was able to prolong or cut short the supreme crest as she chose. Miss Blanche stretched out the operation until she had completely drained her miserable lover. It was only when she saw him lean back his head and yawn that she consented to stop.

"Oh, oh, my Sporio is easily tired today. He must have squandered his largesse on new loves. Is your black lovely as captivating as I? Or is it her charming little mistress who inspires your passions?"

"Well, why not?" he retorted defiantly. "But until now, I have seen no sign that she has even noticed me. Now that you bring the matter up, I am going to think up some ways to get close to her. You have to admit, my darling, that she is a choice piece."

"Sporio, you are wicked, but I think you are only teasing me when you say such things. I can't understand what you see in her. She doesn't have a brain in her head."

"Bravo, Blanche, I was sure that you would have a dig at her. But just be patient, and you won't lose anything by it," Sporio replied.

When I told the Captain all that I had seen and heard, he contentedly rubbed his hands together and swore that he would be present at my side during one of those amusing language lessons.

But with the absence of his first mate, the poor Captain's duties were double, and the visits he was

147

in the habit of making me in my stateroom had become rarer and rarer. But that evening, since the sea was calm and the wind steady, he found time to give me a few moments.

Because of my vivid description of the hanky-panky between Sporio and Blanche, the Captain showed himself more generous than ever with his amative tokens.

He began by throwing me on my back with my cunt brightly illuminated by the light of the lamp. Then taking a position between my spread thighs, he made me one of those *minettes* a sensitive cunt will never forget. Raising my by the buttocks, he did an incomparable rose-leaf on me with his tongue penetrating to the bottom of the narrower of the orifices. To stimulate him more, I agitated my clitoris by myself. Excited to the point of madness, I was on the verge when, lifting himself up suddenly, he slammed his arrogant prick into the burning tissue of my yearning hollow. No sooner had he finished there than he made the same successful attack on the adjoining aperture. Of course, I made no resistance.

This last assault brought us to the zenith of bliss. While I felt his gland throb in my entrails and inundate me with its hot voluptuous liquid, he feasted his eyes on the crimson beauties of my cunt shuddering with voluptuous spasms.

Soon Sporio realised that the best way to ingratiate himself with me was to cultivate my maid, whom he showered with gifts and promised everything under the sun if she would use her influence with me on his behalf.

It goes without saying that she accepted his proposal and immediately began to plead his cause, less in the hope of some recompense than from her inclination to assist in all matters having to do with sex.

She began by telling of the deep admiration he had for me, and then she tried to inflame my imagination with a lyrical description of his fine manners and the elegant and savant way he was able to manipulate his instrument.

"Oh, my dear mistress, you have no idea how soft his eyes are when he talks about you. His hands are like velvet. Just the touch of them would make you thrill all over. And his prick, his prick! You would die of pleasure at its size and hardness. But at the same time it is so limber and supple. You do not know what you are missing if you do not let him fondle your pussy. It is sheer bliss when his gentle hands begin to open the lips that are moist with joy. You'll go out of your mind when he inserts the radiant head into the mouth and you feel his derriere bouncing up and down as he caresses you as if he were drunk. There is no fucker in the world his equal. He is incomparable. Try him just once, I beg of you, and you will see for yourself that what I say is only a feeble description of what it really is to be with him."

All the while she was talking, the quadroon never left off a moment agitating my clitoris which was becoming burning hot with impassioned desires.

"Oh, Zilla, you're the devil's advocate. What enthusiasm! I bet you completed your apprenticeship with Cupid himself. Well, let's assume for the moment that I agree to your proposal. How will you bring it off?"

"Well, that's the stumbling block. If Mademoiselle Stanhope gets the slightest whiff of it, there'll be fire and brimstone. She'd be capable of setting the ship ablaze. But I have an idea. If you promise not to get angry, I'll tell you it."

"You need not worry about that, Zilla," I assured her. "Now come and tell me what you have in mind."

"Well, I think the best place to meet Sporio is in the salon after everybody has retired to his state-room. The thing is quite feasible if we do it the way I am going to tell you. For some time now, the Captain has had his eye on me, and I would be stupid indeed if I did not realise what he's after. I am sure that, with your permission, of course, if I grant him what he wants, he will not refuse Sporio's request to stay in the salon as late as he wants. Under those conditions, nothing will be easier than to meet him there without any fear of interruption," she finished.

"Well, Zilla, that is well thought out, and as you say, it is not impossible of execution. But what an insatiable woman you are! So now you have to have the Captain. If I don't keep an eye on you, you'll soon have the entire crew down to the cabin-boy. Now that I come to think of it, maybe you have already. In any case, I wouldn't be surprised. But be careful. With so many pricks, there could be an undesirable aftermath."

The little hussy broke out into a roar of laughter.

"No need to worry, Mistress," she retorted with a saucy glint in her eyes. "You know the old saying that there is safety in numbers. And besides, do we know *all* the varieties of pleasure?"

All I could do was to follow her example and laugh along with her.

"That's enough for now," I told her, wiping the

tears from my eyes. "I'll think it over and let you know my decision."

CHAPTER XI

THE TRIUMPH OF SPORIO

After Zilla had gone, I began to ponder what she had told me.

To be honest, I personally felt no repugnance at the thought of an amorous engagement with the Governor's valet. He was a handsome chap, and I had to admit that his manners were those of a gentleman. And Blanche's haughtiness towards me was a powerful stimulant not to refuse him my favours. Really, what piqued me was less the prospect of enjoying myself with the Italian than the malicious pleasure of getting back at the English-woman. A female always enjoys vengeance, and the opportunity seemed just right.

Nevertheless, before committing myself, I deemed it wise to consult first my advisor and mentor, the Captain, and ask his opinion.

At the first opportunity, I told him in the same glowing terms as Zilla the supposed talents of the lackey. I passed over in silence her intentions with regard to him, but I praised her good nature and her sultry temperament. I was not surprised when he informed me that he, too, had noted these very qualities. Nobody was so good a judge of women as my old friend.

The prospect of Zilla did not seem to displease him, for he apparently regarded my plan with a favourable eye.

Stroking his beard, he said thoughtfully: "I'm not going to stand in your way. Besides, he's a very agreeable and pleasant young man and obviously quite suited to give you enjoyment. But don't you find the matter a little difficult to arrange?"

It was then that I informed him of my clever maid's strategem, that is, permitting Sporio to come to the salon after everyone had left it and when all the doors would be closed.

"I wouldn't be surprised if Zilla were with him," I added. "It would give you the chance to spend some time with her alone."

This conclusion to my peroration won me victory. From that moment on, he seemed more impatient than Sporio himself and ordered me to have Zilla prepare everything for that very night.

"And don't forget to tell Zilla to be sure and be there," he said in a stern voice.

I hurried to Zilla and told her the result of the talk I had with the Captain. Overjoyed, she hastened to bear the good news to Sporio.

Immediately, the latter's attitude towards me was completely different. Every time he passed me, he made a deep bow accompanied by a suggestive look in his deep black eyes which, I noticed for the first time, were most attractive and intelligent. He went so far as to serve me a cup of tea before supper and address a few words to me in Italian.

Smilingly, I shook my head to let him know that I did not understand.

"That's true," he said. "I forgot that the Signorina does not know my language."

"I'm sorry that I do not for I understand that it is a lovely tongue."

"Yes, Italian is beautiful, rich in expressions and forms. If the Signorina would deign to do me the honour of accepting, I would be greatly honoured to give her instruction."

"Why not, and I thank you," I easily replied. "But it is not as easy as it sounds. We have few chances of meeting each other, and here we are almost at the end of our voyage. Would you like to start the first chance we have to be alone? If I am not mistaken, I have a volume of your immortal Boccaccio, and it would please me to know, little though it may be, something about his writings."

"I would be more than happy, Signorina. Perhaps you would have a few moments free this evening," he suggested, his eyes addressing me with a mute but eloquent prayer.

Inclining my head in acquiescence, I replied: "Yes, if the weather remains fine." With a nod, he let me know he understood.

It went on that way every day. Zilla came that evening into my stateroom to carry out her functions. She had taken special care with her toilette and appeared more dashing than she usually did. On several occasions she showed her impatience by stamping her foot because old Mrs Stanhope and her daughter were lingering so long in the salon. Finally, they retired, leaving the Captain alone at the table with his maps and compass.

As soon as they were gone, she hurried to him and cunningly asked when he thought we would arrive in Trinidad.

"Day after tomorrow, probably in the afternoon," he replied. Then he asked her if she would like to see on the map exactly where we were.

"Very much so," she enthusiastically said as she pressed her body, as if to see better, close to his.

"There's Trinidad," he said, pointing to it on the map. "We are about fifty leagues distant." He showed the present location.

As she leaned further over to look, he took her by the waist and drew her to him.

"Sit here on my knees. You'll be more comfortable," the Captain said. "How about a little kiss?"

As she sat on his knees, she exclaimed, "What awful creatures you sailors are." Then she wiped her mouth and scratched her chin as if the beard had tickled her. To cure it, he took the liberty of a second kiss.

"You're too sassy, Captain," she protested. "That's enough. Mam'zelle Regine wants Sporio to give her an Italian lesson this evening. Should I go and tell him to come?"

"Only if you promise to come back."

"I shall, but only if you promise to be good and behave."

With that, she quickly made her escape, returning within a short time with the Italian who had been on pins and needles.

In the meantime, the Captain had rolled up his maps which he brought to his cabin. As she was passing her door, he called to her:

"Come in here, you little she-devil, and leave those two by themselves. Besides, we'll be more comfortable in here."

Making no protest as he dragged her in, she kicked the door shut behind her. I was already in

155

the salon when Sporio came with his volume of Boccaccio. He promptly sat at my side.

"Here is the book as I promised you," he began. "But I hope you will not look upon me as a teacher but as your humblest, and most liege and devoted subject."

I was more than a little surprised at his free and easy manner and self-confidence.

"He is certainly no ordinary flunkey," I said to myself.

Subsequent events proved that I was not mistaken.

"Well spoken, Sporio," I commented as I extended my hand for him to kiss. "I shall do as you request. Now come closer to me and give me some notions of the Italian language. I am particularly anxious to hear how it sounds."

"This is a collection of short stories or novelettes of varying interest and merit that are told in turn by the guests at a merry gathering. Should I start with the first one, or would you prefer to make a choice?" he said as he opened the volume.

"I'll leave it up to you, Sporio, for I am sure that you will choose a droll and amusing one."

"Dioneus is perhaps the most diverting of these raconteurs, and one of his funniest is about an old hermit instructing a young and innocent girl in matters of love."

"Oh, I know that story," I laughed. "I have to agree with you in your opinion. Isn't there another just as amusing?"

"Of course," he replied as he turned to the tenth story of the ninth day. After reading a few paragraphs in Italian so I could hear the sound, he began to translate for my benefit:

"At this time, there lived in Barletta a clever doctor who augmented his fees by attending all the fairs held in his province. On one of his trips, he struck up a friendship with a wandering peddler named Pietro who came from Tresanti. Often they travelled together, and whenever Pietro came to Barletta, the doctor never failed to offer him the hospitality of his modest home.

"Pietro was even poorer than the Doctor. His entire fortune consisted of a humble shack in the village of Tresanti. It was just big enough to lodge him, his good-hearted young wife, and his ass. One day, when business brought the Doctor to Pietro's town, the merchant led him to his hearth where he did his best to pay back the cheer he had received in Barletta.

"When it came time to go to bed, Pietro, to his great regret, was unable to offer all the comforts he would have wished. Indeed, the only place to sleep was a narrow bed which he shared with his wife. Consequently, Barolo offered to go to the stable where he would take his repose at the side of his donkey.

"Having been told of the hospitality her husband had received from the Doctor, the wife offered to go and sleep with a woman friend so that he could have the single bed to himself. But the Doctor adamantly refused, saying he did not mind sleeping in the stable with his friend.

" 'My dear Madame Gemmata,' he concluded, 'please do not put yourself out for me. I have to tell you that my mare is not an ordinary animal. Whenever I want, I can change her into a lovely girl who gives me the greatest pleasure. Then, when we have to get back on the road, I transform her back into her original shape. As you can imagine, I am always reluctant to be separated from her.'

"Although she was extremely astonished, the young woman believed every word. Shaking her husband in their bed, she told him what she had just heard.

" 'If Barolo is as good a friend as you say, why don't you ask him to teach you his magic and show you how to change me into a mare? That way, you could do double business with added transportation. You would earn a lot more, and when you got back home, you would turn me back into a woman such as I am now.'

"Pietro, who was as innocent in such matters as his wife, thought it was an excellent idea, and he began to worm the secret out of his friend.

"Barolo, who realised what the simple soul was after, stimulated his curiosity by pretending to dissuade him from trying the experience and telling him that he was out of his mind. But the peddler insisted, begging his friend not to refuse him.

" 'Well, Pietro, since both you and your wife have your hearts set on it, I'll do it. But we all have to be up before dawn tomorrow morning, at which time I'll let you in on the secret. As you will see, the hardest part is the placing of the tail.'

"Pietro and his wife slept poorly that night, so anxious were they to start the magical operation. While it was still dark, they went to awaken the Doctor.

"Barolo, clad only in his shirt, accompanied them back to the house, where he began by saying: 'You are the only ones to whom I shall have confided my secret. The reason why I am doing so is that I want to be agreeable and because you are so eager to know it. If you are sincerely interested in having this experiment succeed, you have to follow my instructions without question no matter how odd they may seem to you.'

"They solemnly promised to obey his orders blindly and do what he told them. Then Barolo placed a candle in his friend's hand, saying: 'Now, Pietro, look carefully at what I am going to do and do not miss a word of what I am going to say. Above all, I forbid you to utter a sound, no matter what meets your eyes. If you do, the spell will be broken.'

"With that, he ordered Gemmata to strip herself of all her clothing until she stood before him completely nude. Then he commanded her to get down on all fours as if she were a mare.

"The Doctor then began to run his hand on the head and face of the young woman as he intoned: 'Let this be the head of a fine mare!' and stroking the hair, 'And may this be the mane of a fine mare.'

"Examining her arms and legs, he cried: 'These will be the legs and hooves of a good mare.' With his lascivious fingers, he fondled the firm and voluptuous dangling breasts, he added: 'And these are the udders of a superb mare!'

"Always repeating the same formula and the same words, he passed his hand over the satiny skin of the simple woman's stomach, guided them to between the rounded thighs which he spread open as far as he could. Then, with lubricious touches, he investigated with greedy eyes her magnificent rump and the adjoining charms.

"At that moment, Pietro, impatient at the slowness of the operation, raised his candle and regarded curiously as the expert fingers went through the fertile valley, abode of pleasure and love, which was enclosed between two superb hemispheres and divided by two lips concealing the scarlet interior. The little button was quivering madly, indicating desire.

"The poor husband had less cause to rejoice than his wife who seemed not bored in the slightest. But he was so frightened by the Doctor's injunction that he dared not say a word lest the experiment not succeed. Consequently, he kept his peace.

"Now came the most difficult part, the affixing of the tail, which was the Doctor's eagerest desire, but there was nothing on Gemmata that could be metamorphosised into a tail. Consequently, he felt obliged to make use of his own resources.

"But I feel embarrassed at continuing," Sporio murmured with downcast eyes. "I'll continue, only if you say so."

"Go on," I commanded him, all my senses aroused.

Throwing aside the book, he leaped from his chair, kneeled before me, and insinuated himself between my legs. One hand retrieved the volume and the other rested on my calf as he continued.

"Barolo then lifted his shirt and grasping the muscle which characterises the masculine sex he planted it with a sudden jab . . .

"Yes, my adored queen, to the stupefaction of the poor husband, the Doctor plunged his member in the welcoming cavern which was near the spot where the tail should sprout. The receptacle was just like yours, my dear Regine. Open, my beloved, those pillars, guardians of the gates of felicity. How sweet and good you are. Now lean back a little. Heavens, the beauties that greet my eyes. What an intoxicating aroma is exhaled from the adorable opening. Please allow me to put my mouth on those lips of honey and suck that little rosy button which is your clitoris which is timidly raising its head. Ah, the sweet slit of love, abode of delight . . . temple of pleasure . . . who could ever underestimate your power? Oh, Regine, your cunt will be paradise for me. My dove. My angel. My treasure. My love. My goddess, let me penetrate into it."

With one arm, he embraced me tightly, and with the hand of the other, he guided the flamboyant head of his feverish organ.

Then he ran the tip from the top to the bottom of my redoubt which was excited to the highest pitch. For several instants, he paused at the entrance. Ah, what a wonderful moment! With one sudden jab, he was in, the weapon stabbing me through. Now it was at the very bottom of me and resting on my matrix. After he had shoved it in as far as he could and it was safely imprisoned in my interior, I felt his swollen testicles bounce against the orbs of my buttocks.

"Oh, my dearest, the fondest of my vows has been realised. I am holding Regine in my arms. My prick is quivering in her adored cunt. My balls are making friends with the rounded cheeks of her derriere. I am devouring her lips with my hot kisses. She's mine. She's all mine. I have her. Drunkenly, I am fucking her. With voluptuousness and frenzy, I am fucking her."

Each time that he repeated that sacred word, his prick jabbed me and his testicles were squeezed against my buttocks.

My cunt had had already several pricks of comparable size, but never had I been so richly

161

nourished. I had no idea of relinquishing that cornucopia until I had exhausted it.

Our sighs were blending when the joyous moment of the climax arrived. Swooning in each other's arms, we rejoiced in that state of prostration which always follows excessive bliss.

"My adored queen, are you satisfied with the devotion your slave showed you?"

Smiling tenderly, I almost mewed like a contented cat.

"Oh, Sporio, fuck me again. Once more. I wish you could fuck me forever without ever stopping."

As if acting on unspoken orders, the membranes of my cunt again tightened around that incomparable prick. This produced another amorous flame in his eyes.

"Oh, carissima, I have had other women, but you have given me more pleasure than all of them put together. I have gone into many cunts, but never one like yours which is worthy of a monarch. It alone is the sanctuary of love."

As he recommenced his slow in-and-out motion, he continued:

"While we go on with our delightful game, I think I should tell you something about myself. Although I am at the moment reduced to the status of a lowly servant, I am the last of one of the noblest families of Florence.

"I was only a boy of twelve when my older brother inherited the title and the fortune. He treated me so harshly and made life so miserable for me that I ran away from home and became a sailor.

"My first ship was one that made the Cuba run. After several crossings, I was taken on by pirates.

During one encounter, with the coastguard, several of the latter were killed and a price was put on our heads. Making my way to Jamaica, I placed myself under the protection of the English government, but it was not long before I fell on hard days. Consequently, I gladly accepted the position I enjoy today with Sir Stanhope, who knew something of my melancholy odyssey. And I must say that he has shown himself most understanding and indulgent towards me, giving me time to continue my studies. And I have taken advantage of his kindness. Since I fled my brother's house, I have learned Spanish and, as you can see, I know enough English to get by."

Just at that moment, the ship suddenly tilted. This was followed by a noise that sounded as if a tempest had overtaken us.

Half-dressed, the Captain rushed out of his cabin, took a quick glance at the barometer, and yelling that a severe hurricane was in the offing, he dashed up the stairs to the pilot-house followed by Sporio.

CHAPTER XII

CAPTURED BY PIRATES

Indeed, a devastating typhoon had broken suddenly without any advance warning as is so often the case in the tropics. When the Captain reached the bridge, he found himself amid the most incredible confusion. Before the crew could hoist the sails, the main mast and jib had been snapped like toothpicks. Now the crippled ship was nothing but a plaything of the wind and the waves.

Sporio offered his assistance and soon proved that he was an able and solid seaman.

After much effort, the crew was able to get rid of the debris encumbering the manoeuvres and the ship was now under some measure of control. But the violence of the storm was such that it was impossible to consider fighting against it. The captain saw no alternative but to let the ship go with the wind.

In the salon, everything was terror, disorder, and confusion. Lady Stanhope and her daughter were sobbing in the arms of one another. The sea poured in through the opened hatchways. The lamps had gone out and we were in water up to our knees with everything that was not solidly bolted down floating and knocking against us.

Eventually, the ship righted itself somewhat. With Zilla's help, I could relight the lamps and re-establish some order.

From time to time, Sporio or the Captain descended to assure us that there was nothing more to fear. The worst of the tempest was over, and the crew was busy repairing the damage.

The afternoon of the following day, the storm had completely passed just as suddenly as it broke. The Captain soon saw that we had been blown far off our course and that we were near the coast of Mexico. He and his men exerted every effort to put things to right.

Sporio showed that he was an invaluable aid in this time of distress. The Captain was delighted with him, and he declared to the Governor that, with his permission, he would make him his first mate.

But soon there was to occur the saddest and most sombre event of my relatively peaceful chequered career. In the calm of the following night when the crew was taking a well-earned rest after so many arduous labours, we were run alongside by two sloops manned by pirates armed to the teeth.

From a distance, they had spotted the precarious condition of our schooner, and, taking advantage of the low-hanging clouds, they had been able to get close to us without our notice.

The Captain and the duty officer put up a heroic resistance, but soon they were overcome by sheer numbers, and my good old valiant loyal friend was killed attempting to defend those for whom he was responsible. Alas, such is life.

Then commenced an indescribable series of orgies, violence, and outrage. Don Pedro, for that was the name of the buccaneer chief, had quickly ascertained the number and station of the women aboard as well as the rank and function of Sir Charles Stanhope.

In a long discourse which was a mixture of poor Spanish, old-fashioned phrases, and Yankee curses, he informed the Governor that he was holding him prisoner until the English government paid a handsome ransom. As for the women, they were a part of his prize. No harm would come to them and they would be treated well as long as they showed themselves properly submissive to him and his henchmen.

"But remember, ladies," he cried, turning to us and cursing like a trooper, "if you put up the least resistance, I'll blow your brains out or make you walk the plank."

As if to prove his point, he fired his pistol over our heads which so frightened us that we hurled ourselves at his feet. After having the Governor tied to a sofa, he ordered his men to seize Lady Stanhope and strip off her clothes.

With tears streaming down her cheeks, she begged them to spare her, but it was wasted effort. Deaf to her cries and wails, they only let up when they had ripped off the last veil of modesty. All she had on was her shoes. Dragging her to the centre of the salon, they bound her hands above her head and attached the rope to a ring hanging from the ceiling.

Don Pedro contemplated her with the eye of a connoisseur, and with an oath in Spanish, he declared that the nanny-goat was better than he had dared hope.

Do I have to tell you that I, too, was astonished? I knew that she had a fresh complexion and a luscious figure, but I had never suspected that her white skin was so satiny. Her stomach was rounded without a trace of a wrinkle. Perhaps it was slightly prominent, but it was embellished at the bottom with a luxurious furpiece of jet black which adorned the space between her thighs. What struck me above all was her derriere. Not only were the globes firm and opulent, but they glistened like fresh milk. I swear that I have never in my life seen such an incomparable bottom.

Then the order was issued to treat the daughter in a like manner. Poor Blanche! Sobbing and trembling with fright, she stuck to me like glue. Our common misery had brought us together. Her ridiculous hauteur had vanished as she bewailed her fate.

"Regine, help me, I beg you. Save me. What should I do?"

I did my best to comfort her, but there was little I could do.

"Alas, my poor friend. We have no choice, it seems, but to submit and make the best of an unfortunate situation."

As the pirates laid their hands on Blanche, one of them, whose name I gathered was Carlo, bent over to my ear and in an almost imperceptible voice, he whispered: "Don't put up any resistance. Keep your chin up and have hope and confidence." In a still lower tone, he added with a significant glance: "Sporio."

At those cheering words, my congealed blood began to flow and my heart beat again.

"Oh, I know that Sporio will come to our rescue. I'll have courage to put up with anything as long as I know we shall be saved."

Blanche resisted more violently than her mother had. While they were pulling off her panties and shift, she never let up scratching and biting her persecutors. Don Pedro was sneering maliciously as he watched the lively scene. On his face was an expression of satanic joy.

"All right," he shouted to his men. "Throw her on her back on the table and spread her legs. I'm going to fuck her, or, I should say, do her the honour of my prick in the presence of her mother and father. But first, let the old bugger feast his eyes on his daughter's cunt and behind. Poor fellow. I bet the last time he saw them was when she was still a suckling."

Sturdy arms brought the wretched girl before Sir Charles, who could not help but see the richly shaded hollow spreading across between the thighs. To tell the truth, the dear man did not appear to feel that he was being harshly punished by being forced to look at his daughter's nudity.

"Now, boys, make him kiss the cunt and stick his nose in the girl's perfume bottle."

The brutes lifted Blanche so that her two jewels were directly in front of her father's face, and then they ran them up and down from his nose to his mouth.

I do not want to make a hasty judgment, but I thought I saw the old scoundrel smacking his lips as if the taste and odour were eminently agreeable and delicious.

"Rest her now on the table, and bring me that little thing," (poor I!) he commanded. "We'll see what she has to offer when she is naked."

"Pardon!" I said calmly as they were about to put their hands on me. "I do not need any help. I can undress myself."

From the corner of his eye, Carlo gave me an approving look, while I unperturbedly rid myself of my finery.

Motioning me to come to him after I stood before him in the state in which I came into the world, he said approvingly: "Indeed you are an appetising piece. Now bring out my belaying pin and let it see the light of day."

I have to admit that I understood very well what the wretch was saying and here is why. I had learned a little Spanish Creole, the dialect he was speaking, from two fugitive slaves that Captain Saint-Jean had found half-dead on the shores of Cuba and whom he turned over to my father. My father treated them well and they became part of the plantation personnel. They were great friends of Zilla, and through them, I picked up some of the Spanish spoken on the islands.

I promptly obeyed. The type of clothing he wore was not unfamiliar to me. First of all, I unrolled the bejewelled belt that imprisoned his waist. Then, unbuttoning his tight-fitting trousers, I took hold of his organ and pulled it out as well as the two inflated sacks of his testicles. Pirate he may have been, but his prick was superb and a stallion would have been proud of his balls.

I could see that he was flattered at the way I looked at the magnificent gland. He was even happier when I began to stroke it, and he was completely won over when I took it between my lips and then in my mouth.

Momentarily amused by these bagatelles, the blackguard went over to the table where his two acolytes continued to hold down Blanche on her back.

With one hand, the poor girl was trying to conceal the seats of her modesty as she gave out lusty kicks with her legs. She clawed and bit any brigand who dared get close enough.

Don Pedro was splitting his sides with uncontrollable humour as he watched her frenzied defence. Coming closer to her, he seized the hand which was veiling her charms and abruptly tore it away. But his laughter quickly turned to furious anger, for the exasperated English girl, with a force one would have not thought her capable of, boxed him so soundly on the ear that the ring was heard all over the salon.

Although they were slightly alarmed, the two aides could not repress their laughter. Pedro, equally astonished at the affront, gave an evil smile and ordered her to be turned on her stomach.

Then, rolling up his sleeves, he began to administer with his powerful hands a formidable spanking on Flamingo's buttocks. The poor backside turned almost immediately to a deep red.

That was the moment the buccaneer was waiting for. Unceremoniously opening the flaps of the cunt whose interior was a dazzling scarlet, he inserted into it his impressive organ with a single jab and began to fuck her with his testicles swaying from side to side.

This treatment seemed to have for effect the calming of Blanche's wrath. She stopped trying to fight back and accepted without further struggle what she obviously had come to regard as inevitable. Judging from the spasms of her bottom, she did not seem to find the humiliation too disagreeable.

As soon as he had discharged, he withdrew his still irritated gland, sat down for a moment's rest, and summoned one of his cohorts, a one-eyed criminal named Federigo, to whom he cynically said: "Old fellow, I know your preference for juicy omelettes, so you can take my place."

Federigo did not have to be told twice. Throwing himself on Blanche, he soon proved himself a worthy successor to his superior in the receptacle brimming over with his sperm.

I waited for her screams, but in vain. There was not a sound to be heard from her. Indeed, she appeared to be taking the second attack better than the first. But what seemed even stranger to me was the way her mother was following eagerly with her eyes the rising and falling buttocks of Federigo pumping the overheated receptacle of her daughter.

While this was going on, Don Pedro, who did not like to be idle, led me to the Governor with the order to take his prick and make it stand up. Again, I complied immediately. Kneeling before Sir Charles, I caressed and kissed the dear old thing that I knew so well. At a fresh order, I raised my rump while the pirate chief told Carlo that if he wished, he could fuck me from behind.

Hurriedly, Carlo came to kneel behind me. Enwrapping me with his arms, he supported himself on my derriere and inserting his powerful engine in my interior, he mumbled in my ear:

"With pleasure, Mam'zelle, but I'll fuck you only with your formal permission."

"Go right ahead, Carlo," I answered. "You're not too bad, and it might as well be you as another."

Sir Charles could not suppress a smile as he heard that. Aroused by the caresses I was bestowing on him, he told me gently:

"You are a brave girl with a lot of good sense, Regine. You know that you have to submit, willy-nilly, to your fate, and you try to reap some advantage from adversity itself."

His prick, now in full erection, was abundant proof that with him, bad luck had not stifled his erotic faculties. It was literally throbbing in my fingers, while its owner with a concupiscent eye was watching Carlo fucking me like a gentleman from behind. It was a matter of seconds before the bucca-neer was flooding me with his hot liquid and at the precise instant when Federigo, groaning with lust, spurted into the already generously moistened crevice of Blanche.

It is well known that the greater the raptures, the greater the ensuing fatigue. When the last shudder had coursed through our bodies and shaken our frames and the pricks and cunts were drained of their contents to the last drop, we all, with deep sighs, fell back in swoons and went asleep in the outrageous positions in which Morpheus had placed us. It was a well-earned rest.

As we came to, I detached my sluggish hand from poor Sir Charles's drooping member. Over-whelmed by what he had enjoyed, Don Pedro sent Carlo to fetch us the best wines to be found in the holds.

Here would be a good place to pause momentarily to clarify what happened next and to recount events that I knew nothing about until only later.

After the brief struggle which took place on the bridge, during which the pirates took firm control of the schooner, the victors had tied hand and foot the crew members and locked them up in the prow.

Sporio was only a servant and as such of possible use to them, either by getting the finest vintages for them or ferreting out the money. In any case, Sporio was given his liberty.

As old friends, Carlo and Sporio had recognised each other immediately. Under the pretext of showing the former where the Governor's strongbox was, the Italian took him to a secluded nook where they embraced each other warmly.

In the course of their brief conversation, Carlo declared that his present way of life was hateful and he would give anything to be free of it.

Leaping at the chance, Sporio told him that deliverance was possible. If only he would assist him saving the Governor, he could be assured of a full pardon for his past transgressions as well as a munificent compensation. He was so eloquent that his old comrade was persuaded with the condition that his fellow cut-throats' lives would be spared.

Sporio began to make his plan which consisted of getting the pirates drunk on wines and liqueurs which would be dosed with certain drugs. Then they would be put back on their ships and brought to Trinidad. Nothing was simpler or easier. Sporio had been placed in charge of the Governor's pharmacy which was plentifully supplied with laudanum, morphine and other narcotics. And

Carlo was charged with delivering the message into my ear and keeping a protective eye on me.

All I have just now told took place within a few instants before Carlo returned to us in the company of Don Pedro.

Like birds of prey, the humbler members of the pirate crew had swooped down on Zilla and Miss Stanhope's maid. The latter, who put up a fierce resistance, underwent unmentionable outrages from which she suffered seriously. Zilla, bending her head to the wind, fared much better. Aided by her natural inclinations, she did what was expected of her and emerged relatively unscathed.

Stripping off her clothes, they ran their hands over her body, made a minute inspection of her person, and tossed her this way and that in every sense of the word.

They sucked her cunt. They sucked her asshole. They fucked her from behind, in the front, on top, and on bottom. She manipulated their pricks and she sucked them, too. She fondled their balls and licked their bottoms. She was so successful and found so much favour that with one voice the sea-robbers declared she was the most luscious and desirable female in the entire Caribbean.

Notable, too, were her staying powers. She later told me that she had lost count after the twenty-fifth time, and for more than two hours, her mouth, cunt and hands were never empty of pricks.

In my opinion, if a woman wishes to escape serious harm, all she has to do is submit.

While the pirates were giving themselves up to such excesses, Sporio kept plying them with strong drinks laced with powerful drugs. Gradually, one by one, the revellers felt the effects of voluptuous-

174

ness and drink and dropped off into profound slumbers.

Now let us return to the final scene in the salon. We remember that Don Pedro had sent Carlo in search of liquid refreshment. Carlo hastened to obey. Returning with Sporio, he had with him a case of superior rum, the oldest of the old, "Old Tom." While one was setting up the glasses, the other was uncorking the bottles.

When he placed a glass before me, Sporio murmured: "Don't drink it. Just pretend to, but, by all means, encourage the pirates to drink as much as they can."

At that time, I did not know what he meant by the warning, but since he now enjoyed my full confidence, I relayed the information to Sir Charles and my companions in misery.

Don Pedro and his lieutenants invited us to keep them company. Bringing our glasses to our lips, we merely moistened our tongues with the alcohol. Carlo and Sporio were indefatigable in filling the empty cups. It did not require much encouragement on their part since our captors were gulping down bumpers as if suffering from insatiable thirsts. After a short time, the narcotics took effect. Heads sagged and sleep closed their eyes.

The moment for action had finally come. Sporio and Carlo began by collecting the arms of the drunken sea-marauders and then tightly bound Don Pedro to Federigo with stout cords. As they were thus busily engaged, we women, trembling and nervous, hastily re-donned the garments we had been deprived of.

Then our two saviours took care of the rest of the motley crew. Those keeping watch on the bridge were also sound asleep, and as they were snoring, Zilla disarmed them, too. All that were left were a few guards on the poopdeck and in the life-boats. They had all drunk their fill with the exception of one who persisted in his abstinence.

As an explanation, he said that he had recently killed one of his mates in a brawl while under the influence of alcohol, and although he was absolved by the others, he made a vow to his patron saint that never again would he touch a drop.

Zilla was in despair. But Sporio consoled her by telling her to take him a cup of coffee which was heavily dosed with morphine. She lost no time in going to the teetotaller on whom she employed all her considerable charms and wiles. She could not bear to be away from him, the cunning miss told him, and the coffee she had for him was a token of her affection. How could he resist? The beverage was soon downed with the drug working almost immediately.

Finally, they were all dead to the world. One by one, they had been overcome by the soporifics. Now, trussed like chickens, they were returned to their barks and laid under the benches. We left them with only two oars so that they could not pursue us. Then we cut the cables loose, abandoning them to their own resources and the grace of God.

Our own crew had been freed as soon as it had been possible to do so without any risks. Putting himself at their head, Sporio hoisted sail to the favourable wind and soon our foes, the pirates, were lost from sight.

With unanimous agreement, Sporio took over command of the ship and made Carlo his second.

Then we headed for Trinidad. He was the hero of the hour.

The Governor showed himself prodigal in his gratitude, and all of us could not express our gratitude sufficiently to Sporio for having saved our lives. And he was universally complimented for his cool head and skill.

Alas, our happiness was of short duration.

Poor Lady Stanhope, who had been suffering from heart trouble for a long time, was unable to recover from the terrors of that awful night. In spite of the care her daughter and I lavished on her and the medicaments supplied by Sporio, the unfortunate woman expired in our arms. The next day, her mortal remains were piously and solemnly given to the sea.

This sad happening brought us still more closely together, Blanche and myself, and cemented the bonds of our friendship. The old Governor resigned himself to his melancholy loss. Along with his daughter, he begged me to accept the hospitality of their roof as long as I was to be on the island.

Sir Charles added that he was going to write my father, requesting that I be permitted to stay with him and be a companion to his daughter. He would take charge of my education.

Without saying a word about it, this offer was the very thing I desired. Consequently, I accepted the kind offer to remain with them until my father's reply was received.

The rest of the voyage passed without incident and we did not come across any more pirates. Finally, we dropped anchor at Port of Spain, the capital of Trinidad.

Then, thanking God for having saved us so

miraculously, we prepared to enjoy once again all the benefits and pleasures that liberty alone can grant us.

THE PANGS OF VENUS

Anonymous

CHAPTER ONE

If Madame Benoit shrugged her shoulders with a knowing look when the purity and austerity of my manner of living was discussed, she had good cause for it.

Madame Benoit was an old friend, a friend of my childhood. About twenty-four years ago she married a tax collector in the little town of N—, where I made the acquaintance of the gentleman whom I called Monseieur Benoit at first, and who simply became Benoit to me afterwards.

My dear friend had the weakness to confide everything to his wife, even to his old love scrapes, which were familiar to her, and that is why Madame Benoit shrugged her shoulders when my wonderful qualities were enumerated.

Benoit had died some years previously and being somewhat lonely in my bachelor quarters, I took an apartment near my late friend's widow.

There was a good deal of whispering to be sure, but Madame Benoit was forty-two years old and I was forty-eight. The fire of youth was probably soon to be extinguished for my neighbour but as for myself, the older I got, the younger I felt.

My time was spent in dressing, eating, and visiting. I rose late. However, if I was in bed even five minutes before eleven A.M. I was up at eleven sharp. It was my rule at five minutes past eleven every day to be in my bath, as I usually took a cold bath in winter as well as in summer.

Fifteen minutes after eleven, I jumped out of the water to be rubbed down by my faithful Jean. This operation lasted ten minutes. Then, warmly enveloped, I gave myself up to the delightful operation of touching up my beard with a dye brush and as I was almost bald, the work was not arduous.

My lady friends only saw me at night when I lit up to great advantage, adding to this that when I was not under the scrutinising eye of Madame Benoit I was very lively, even adventurous, as you will see when you read on.

At noon my toilet was completed and as the clock struck twelve I might have been seen every day rapping at the widow's door.

I generally found one or two callers, not too old, however, to have deserted the ranks of the armchair maids and widows, still on the qui vivre for a husband.

I would chat for a quarter of an hour, and Madame Benoit would give one of her shrugs when fat Mademoiselle Rosalinde would say between two languishing glances: "Ah, how well does Monsieur Dormeuil carry his forty years. It is the effect of regular habits; a well spent existence will bear its fruit."

Naturally I would stammer some polite answer but when Madame shook her head with an "Ough!" I slipped out of the room. How, I could not say. Far from being timid, heaven knows, I cannot yet understand the terror which seized me when I was in the presence of my terrible neighbour and her friend.

I always took my first meal of the day on the corner of the Rue Montmartre where I read the morning papers. This took one hour and a half altogether.

About two o'clock I strolled along the boulevards and there, in a little shop, I sought my sweet scented correspondence. Mademoiselle Hortense, who kept the little shop, was an old acquaintance of mine.

Ah, Hortense was a queer girl! If just for fun, you had a fancy to stoop down near her, and while her handsome dark eyes gazed fixedly into yours, you slipped your hand dexterously under her petticoats, you would find a firm and well shaped leg in a nicely gartered stocking. Following the stocking, which led you far, you would have found the contour of a thigh still half covered by the stocking, but as to the other half—oh! you ask me the feeling one has on such occasions? Oh, nothing, but the devilish sensation which always seizes me when I come in contact with the warm, soft palpitating flesh of a woman!

And Mademoiselle Hortense's flesh was so soft in its firmness! You proceeded to pass your hand gently around her thigh, when all at once to your surprise, you could get no further. It was merely her other fat thigh which pressed closely against this one. And there between, a little upwards, was one of nature's marvels, with a tuft of curly hair hidden away in the midst of the soft silky bush you would find it a little more moist than it had been a moment before.

I touch the slit with my finger and Mademoiselle

Hortense's looks grow more and more sensuous. My finger moved gently upward and inward, when she would open her thighs widely . . .

My trousers become uncomfortable. Mademoiselle throws one arm about my neck and presses tighter and still tighter as my finger moves faster and faster. I feel it slip all the way up the passage, which is in an amorous blaze. It becomes wet!

What is going to happen? Why nothing, it is all over. Mademoiselle Hortense would straighten up all at once and tap on my hand for form's sake. Her look was no longer intense. Pretty soon boxes would be quickly opened. I used to buy in this way, every fortnight on Thursdays, a pair of gloves. I had at one time many pairs of gloves.

It is time that I should return to my deliciously perfumed correspondence. Some days I found it quite voluminous, other days I had none. The day on which I started these memoirs, I found a tiny note awaiting me.

One Thursday for the reason just given, I remained later than usual at Mademoiselle's. On other days I only took the time to get my letters and exchange polite salutations with her.

Happy possessor of a loving message, I left the shop and walked with a quick step as far as the Rue Coq-Herron where I had a small room.

There, lying back in an easy chair, I could, without fear of interruption, devote myself entirely to the charms of a somewhat hazardous literature inspired by a little god called Cupid by some, but whom others insist upon calling Mammon.

Although each day seemed to repeat itself, yet it was always new to us and it was with the same trembling hand that I tore open the delicate envelope, and always with the same kind of emotion that I plunged into the perusal of a dear, capricious letter. I enjoyed at that time a pleasure that no doubt many persons would fail to understand. I unfolded the letter which read thus:

My dear Friend,

I will need you this evening at the Hotel X—. Do not forget your promise of the day before yesterday, or I will pull out—you know . . .

Truly yours
PAULINE

Pauline was a handsome girl but I could not obtain anything from her but correspondence for a long time. I accepted writing to her with the hope that I would gain my point some day, but in vain. You will see later on how I succeeded.

Although it was too early to keep my appointment with Pauline, nevertheless I directed my steps in the direction of the Hotel X—simply because it was my regular hour. When the sweet little maid opened the door, she said mockingly, as she looked at the clock: "I could have guessed it was you!"

The roguish remark was worth the five francs I placed in her hand as I familiarly walked into the little parlour, whose open doors seemed to tender me a pressing invitation. And then I heard the melodious voice of a siren: "Julie!" said the voice, "if Monsieur Lorille comes, bring him in at once."

Julie had no time to answer, as I was already in the room. A splendid blonde was half sitting, half lying on a sofa. I remained standing before her with bowed head. I have always been gallant and I was humbly awaiting when a peal of laughter caused me to start.

"I have not called for a mirror, you are mistaken!"

The little woman was indulging in a hearty laugh at the expense of my bald head. A novice would have been confused, but I answered:

"What, Madame, such charming beauty as yourself, could not do better than admire her own image, she would then imagine that all around her was beautiful."

"Upon my word, Monsieur."

"Monsieur Dormeuil, at your service."

"Monsieur Dormeuil," continued the blonde, "you must forgive me. I like to laugh but I am not the worse for it. Be seated."

Before the charming creature could finish her sentence I was by her side.

"Never having had the happiness to meet you before, Madame, would it be an indiscretion on my part to ask your name?"

"Yes, sir, at least until I know you better."

"To know you better, Madame, is my dearest wish."

"Monsieur Dormeuil," answered the blonde, "men are ungrateful wretches. There is M. Lorille for instance, for whom I have sacrificed so much, but who does not even come as he promised to."

"Adorable blonde, just make half of that same sacrifice for me and . . . "

"What would you have then? I find you rather—what would you call it?" said the little woman impatiently.

"Call it ambitious, that is all!" I replied.

She gave me a look that sent a thrill through my flesh.

By degrees I got nearer to my charmer, I admired her earrings and found her dress in good taste; I wanted to see her shoes, but she refused. However, a well-turned compliment on her dimpled cheeks gained me a smile, which made me notice her beautiful teeth. I tried to kiss my way to them but unsuccessfully.

"Ah, what a beautiful little hand, let me kiss it!" and I obtained permission to do so. Her arm was not withdrawn when I covered it with burning kisses. Little by little, the pretty blonde laughed oftener and easier. Her eyes lighted up; very soon I could see her foot and her ankle —afterwards I was allowed to kiss her cheek. Shyly, I tried to put my lips on her mouth but without success. Finally, on trying again, I not only had a kiss but it was returned.

Liberties now fast succeeded to more serious liberties. I unfastened her waist and feverishly pulled at the fine linen which covered the most beautiful breasts that I had ever seen. My lips wandered from one to the other, and when I had taken off the corset, I seized successively between my teeth, the two little nipples, pink as strawberries.

How good it was to feel those tiny points in my mouth. I leaned over to snatch up the skirts and she offered no resistance. I opened her drawers. Heavens, what beautiful curly hair, and just enough too.

Suddenly I found a little hand trying to find its way into my trousers and with astonishing dexterity my instrument was drawn out, the use of which she seemed so thoroughly to understand in all its details. She gently pulled, and lowered its cap . . .

"I beg of you my dear, stop! Do stop, or I will spend!" I cried as I felt the intense excitement getting the better of me.

"Make haste then and get at my little pet!" she replied, as she pressed my pizzle into the opening of her fragrant bower.

Ah, what a sensation, it was a little tight but how good and soft. I passed my hands under her bottom, voluptuous to the touch, as it rose and fell in my grasp.

Her mouth clung to mine; my tongue caught hers and found it. My little blonde heaved and fluttered and quivered; her tongue pressed harder against mine. Her beautiful breasts, of which I did not lose sight for a moment, palpitated convulsively.

"Oh, go on, it is coming! Not so fast! Faster! Now kiss me—wait—now, there. How good it is! All the way in—all the way in—oh—oh—oh!"

She lifted her bottom, her mouth was glued to mine, the little beauty's body and mine were made but one . . . Then one long shudder with a sharp movement of her buttocks, saying . . . "I am coming . . . go on! quick! Oh, heavens", and she spent. Finally she fell into a spasm of voluptuous rapture. She was beautiful as she lay in her amorous disorder; her hair slightly disarranged, her skirts well raised, showing the wonderful whiteness of her skin.

She remained in this position a moment longer, then rising, she moved towards the door with an unsteady step, unbolted it and passed out of the room without once turning around.

She was probably going to repair the disorder of her toilet and I did the same on my side.

The hall clock struck five when the young woman re-entered the room, sat down in a chair opposite me and looked calmly at me. After a short silence, I said:

"Mademoiselle, or Madame, sit a little nearer and forgive my silence. I am still under the spell your charms have thrown over me."

As she approached, I took her hand and drew her down onto my lap.

"Have you any family, Monsieur Dormeuil?" she finally asked.

I shook my head. "No," I said, surprised at her question.

"I see—you are a horrid old bachelor!" she said with a pout. I bowed, a little flattered.

"Not too old though," she soon added smilingly, "or you might have come off worse than you did. You love to spend your nights in debaucheries, I suppose, like Monsieur Lorille. I must introduce you to that gentleman, he is a dear friend of mine and has related some of his adventures to me.

"He has had many and knows many more, but the one which follows is one of his most entertaining."

CHAPTER TWO

"Not far from the Varennes, on the banks of the Aire," she began in a dreamy way, "stands a convent, in a little valley nestling among the mountains.

"The good nuns there spend their lives in prayer and in sewing for the orphans of the village. Their number, when the convent is full, is about forty. The little church, situated in the middle of the village, counts among its flock the inhabitants of the country for ten miles round and includes the convent in question.

"The officiating priest being old and feeble, was assisted by a young Abbé who had arrived only a few days previous to the opening of this story. The young Abbé was of such modest demeanour, that even the oldest bigots of the parish took him for a saint in swaddling clothes.

"The young girls all remarked that he was undeniably handsome and when they went to the confessional, each one went early to be sure to get a chance to confess during the day.

"The old curate was not sorry to be relieved of his arduous work and it was only right that the poor man should have some rest. He now only confessed the nuns at the convent every fortnight, when they sent their old coach for him.

"It was always a treat at the convent when the venerable priest visited them. They dined in the great refectory and he seemed to bring with him an odour of out-of-doors, which always touched the hearts of the novices, who sighed every now and then under its influence.

"One day, however, the old vehicle brought the young Abbé to the convent. The old curate was ill and had sent his excuses to the Lady Superior. The latter received the young man in the parlour on the ground floor and was quite charmed with his modest bearing. They conversed at first about the curate, then about the crops, then the church. They had been repairing the chapel of St Anthony, etc.

"The Lady Superior finally assembled the nuns in order to present them to their new pastor, and one after another they passed before him and curtsied without raising their eyes to his face. Why should they, since he was only to speak words of peace and comfort to them from behind the wooden grating.

"Three novices were the last to enter. One of them had examined the young Abbé through a crack in the door before coming in, and her cheeks became crimson as she curtsied to him.

"After the presentation the Lady Superior made a little speech and then accompanied the Abbé to the chapel, followed by the whole party of nuns.

"The young priest opened the centre door and closed it carefully after him a moment later. A slight rustling told his auditors that he was slipping on a white surplice that was hanging inside the door, then came the noise of a stool sliding across the floor, and all was silent.

"The nuns were all present except those occupied with the household duties. They had glided into the chapel more like shadows than like human beings. Two of them knelt in the confessional.

"Presently the sound of a deep voice, followed by soft whisperings was heard. The murmur ceased, then commenced again. Then came a long silence. The arms of the sinner moved restlessly as she pronounced mea culpa. The Lady Superior rose with a bowed head, her arms crossed on her breast, moved towards the little chapel of the Holy Virgin.

"All the nuns in turn came and knelt on either side of the confessional. Finally it was the turn of the youngest novice.

"Trembling with fear and yet impatient to hear the Abbé's voice on the other side of the grating, she knelt down on her little wooden stool. By closing her eyes and stopping her ears she tried to examine her conscience. The image of the Abbé, however, would rise up before her. She waited until the rattle of the little window warned her that he was ready to listen to her, and the confession began!

" 'Your blessing, my father,' etc., etc., until the solemn moment arrived when her most secret thoughts must be unveiled.

" 'My child, have you sinned in thought; have you longed for the world and the pleasures thereof?'

"She gave no answer.

"Then the Abbé whispered low: 'Have you ever had any bad thoughts? Did you ever commit any sinful deeds?'

"Still she could not answer.

" 'Have you listened to the demon tempting you

to sensual actions? Speak without fear, my child, God is good and will forgive.'

" 'My father,' stammered the poor little novice, not understanding and yet trying to see the priest who was plying her with these terrible questions.

"She could only distinguish, however, through the grating, two flashing eyes which stirred her very soul with a magnetic influence, which the poor little novice would have been unable to define.

" 'Yes, father!' she replied at last, forced to say something.

" 'Have you sinned in thoughts and deeds, my child. How many times?' he then inquired, his voice trembling slightly. 'Did you commit these sins alone or have you a companion in sin? Speak, my child, to obtain pardon, you must confess all, as you can only obtain peace after a full confession. Have you given yourself up to Satan by day or by night? Be careful not to commit sacrilege. I shall be obliged to refuse you absolution the next time if you do. Meanwhile examine your conscience carefully. Pray for help. Then you can approach the communion table. Pray every night with a contrite heart. Go, my child!'

"With an unsteady step she left the chapel. That night the young nun, Sister Clemence by name, could not sleep. She tossed restlessly on her narrow bed, and could think of nothing but the words the Abbé had spoken.

" 'Sinned in thoughts—yes, often I have longed to leave the convent and enter the beautiful shops in the city. Then there was Mr Ernest, who used to come to my aunt's house. I have often thought how delightful it would be to ramble through the woods with him alone. But are these bad thoughts—sensual thoughts?' she said.

"She finally closed her eyes and fell asleep and saw Satan! Yes, it was Satan. All at once, however, he assumed the form of the Abbé.

"He took her hand and placed it between her legs. Oh, what a delicious sensation, how delightful. 'Mr Satan, Mr Abbé, please, please go on . . . don't stop . . . ah, this is delicious! . . . oh! . . . Mr Abbé!!'

"Sister Clemence awoke suddenly, trembling like a leaf, weak and tired. She felt numb between her legs. Placing her hand there, she found it was wet . . . poor little novice, she could not understand.

"Daylight appeared at last, but Clemence was unable to rest. She threw back the coverings and raised her long white chemise. She wanted to see, but there was nothing but the little stain of blood which surprised her very much at this particular time of month.

"When the great bell gave the signal for rising, Sister Clemence, usually so quick and lively, crept out of bed with difficulty and dressed herself slowly. She was the last to enter the chapel and kneeling down, joined her hands mechanically for the morning prayer.

"In the refectory she was unable to eat. When the Lady Superior arrived she questioned her. She was a sort of physician but she perceived nothing extraordinary in the symptoms of her subordinate and advised a few days of rest.

"During the eight days that Sister Clemence remained in her cell, she did not seem to improve; on the contrary, she grew worse and worse. She could not sleep and if she happened to fall into

194

a feverish slumber, the same vision pursued her, accompanied by the same temptations. It sometimes happened that even half awake, her hands would seek the mysterious spot, centre of such delightful sensations, and unconsciously her fingers lingered there.

"Finally, entirely awake, the same irresistible power drew her fingers to the same place, but then it required a longer time to reach the point of supreme enjoyment.

"At first the novice's thoughts were not fixed upon any particular object. Then she thought of Mr Ernest, and lastly of the Abbé. What a sacrilege!

"If you had seen this little childish hand buried between those white thighs, smooth and firm as marble, her lovely eyes partly closed and those ripe red lips slightly parted, you would have seen her body motionless at first, become slightly agitated, then the legs move further and further apart, the little finger slip in and out of the rosy mouth, until with a deep sigh, she sank back, powerless to move hand or foot.

"Two weeks had elapsed and the Abbé returned to confess the nuns. The Lady Superior called on the invalid and asked her if she wished to confess. She even said that the Abbé had kindly offered to come to her cell as she was not able to rise. How to thank the Abbé for such a favour!

" 'Certainly, Mother, I should like to confess,' dutifully replied Sister Clemence.

"The Lady Superior left the cell and soon returned with the Abbé who entered with that bearing of humility he habitually assumed. He appeared most concerned at the illness of the novice and insisted that a full confession was the best possible remedy.

"Sister Clemence did not dare look at him, she was so confused. The Lady Superior retired, and the Abbé took a chair by the side of the bed.

" 'Have you examined your sinful heart, my child; are you ready to make a full confession?'

" 'Yes, my father!'

"The confession began. The poor little Sister did not know how to reveal what had happened. The fear, however, of not receiving absolution and communion gave her courage. She disclosed everything.

"The Abbé drew closer and closer, until she felt his breath upon her face. Her eyes were closed.

"Suddenly she felt his lips pressing hers in a long kiss. Unconsciously, a timid little kiss from her lips answered his. Then she felt a warm hand upon her body, which gradually seemed to move downward towards that spot where Satan had placed her finger on a certain night.

"The Abbé took another kiss, his hand passed gently over her thighs and slipping under her bottom, forced her to turn over on her side. Now he slapped her gently and pushed his finger into her slit between the two hills of her bottom, and it finally found its way into what appeared to be his desire to reach.

"But his hand set everything on fire on its way. With the other hand he unbuttoned his robe, undid his trousers and pulled out a prick whose erection was fully justified by the beauties his hand had explored and was still exploring.

"With a sudden pull, to throw off the cover, he laid himself down on the edge of the couch, close

to her. Then, pressing her in his arms he covered
her lips with kisses and taking her hand, placed it
upon his god of love, firm and rigid as a rock.

"The contact caused the novice to open her eyes.
He called her by the most endearing names: 'My
love, open your eyes—kiss me. Open your
eyes—receive my tongue—give me yours—so! Do
you know what you are holding and squeezing so
hard, my dear? It is the tree of life that you have so
often heard about and desired so ardently without
knowing the reason why. Place it where you put
your finger sometimes. There! Not so quick! Open
your legs . . . one minute . . . there it is!' and the
enormous instrument presented its head to the little
pussy as she instinctively drew nearer to the Abbé.

"He pushed gently, then raising her chemise, he
uncovered her breasts and sucked them, bit them,
then returned to her lips and with a shove he
pushed his prick into its rightful place as he smothered a scream from the poor little novice. Now they
are enlaced in the closest embrace and when his
pizzle seemed to come out, she clung to him; when
she seemed to recede, he boldly followed her up.

"He came out and went in; the action became
accelerated; in her amorous transports she crossed
her beautiful legs over his back and wriggled about
like a dear little eel.

" 'Go on, darling!'

" 'Not so quick!' " 'Do you feel as if you were
coming?'

" 'Yes—it is coming!'

" 'Quick!—your mouth—your tongue!'

" 'Father—oh, how delightful it is. I am
coming—heavens, how big it is once more.'

" 'There!' said the Abbé, panting, as he gave

a last shove. His engine disappeared in the tiny opening.

"Sister Clemence held him in a close embrace and covered his face with grateful kisses for the good he had done her.

"From this day on, the Abbé, who had found means of corresponding with the attractive novice, succeeded in introducing himself into the convent many times and Sister Clemence often found herself amorously wriggling under the vigorous pizzle of the priest.

"She received a thorough education in the Art of Love and soon recovered her health. However, this state of affairs could not last much longer. The Abbé was no more to be made a priest and reside forever in the quiet little village than was Sister Clemence to remain in a convent.

"The old aunt who had brought her up had been an invalid for years and finally died, leaving her a handsome fortune. From that time, the whole convent busied itself in trying to persuade her to take her final vows and give up her fortune to the community.

"The Prior even condescended to come in order to preach to her and the poor little novice was about to accede to their wishes, when the Abbé proposed that they should elope.

"One night he came to the secret door of the convent, carrying under his arm a bundle containing a complete suit of boy's clothing, together with a long cloak. Sister Clemence quickly put them on and together they slipped out of the place unseen.

"The novice looked fairly bewitching in her new costume. She spread her legs however a little too much in walking, and after hurrying along for a couple of miles, the Abbé proposed making an examination to see what the trouble could be between those beautiful legs of hers.

"He made her lean up against a tree and unbuttoned her trousers for her. To handle the lips of her little secret mousetrap was his only object, as you may imagine. He soon had her so excited that he was obliged to put his mouth down to it and with his tongue play a thousand amorous tricks.

"In her voluptuous transport, she sought with feverish hand the Abbé's fiery monster, which was only too gratified at being set at liberty. Seizing it, she stroked it vigorously.

"To describe that scene would be impossible. The Abbé's tongue was well educated. Sliding between those rosy lips of her slit, it suddenly came out to circle itself into a multiple of tongues, so rapid were its movements.

"Meanwhile Sister Clemence shook his wand furiously, convulsively, and the movement of her bottom indicated that her delicious moment was coming.

"The Abbé's tongue went slower but pressed harder, and when she gave him a great shove accompanied by a warm rub on his immense cock, a superb jet spouted from the latter, while he received her little amorous dew upon his tongue, the deserved tribute of conscientious labour.

"That very day the Abbé cast his robe to the four winds of heaven and carried little Sister Clemence off to Paris. Once in possession of her fortune, she took pretty lodgings and furnished them nicely. She made up her mind to have a good time between theatre-going and her amorous sports with the

Abbé, who had also a comfortable income of his own."

"The story of Sister Clemence is excellent, Mademoiselle," said I, "and I would give much to make her acquaintance as well as that of the Abbé. Unfortunately, it is only fiction!" I added.

"On the contrary, it is a story of real life, M. Dormeuil, the true history of a person to whom I can introduce you, if you like," replied the little woman.

"Truly I would be charmed to know her and shall await an introduction with impatience," I answered.

"You will not have long to wait," was the unexpected reply of the blonde. She then rose and making a timid curtsy, her eyes modestly cast down, her hands joined, she said:

"Allow me to introduce to you Sister Clemence, Monsieur Dormeuil," and she broke into a merry laugh.

I was amazed. "And the Abbé?" I inquired.

"You have heard me speak of Monsieur Lorille? He is the Abbé," she answered quietly.

I had a good laugh over the whole adventure, and then we conversed pleasantly on many subjects until we were interrupted by the arrival of Pauline.

Pauline was certainly a very handsome girl, very tall and graceful, with rich brown hair, large full, frank eyes and tiny hands and feet. She was Pauline for everybody here but Madame L. de Portiera for Parisian Society.

There were only a few privileged persons at the Hotel X—who had seen her face. This house was a particularly exclusive one, and only frequented by the elite.

Indiscretion was unkown there. Amuse yourself as much as you like and as long as you like but never overstep the boundaries of good society. Such was the motto and the rule of this remarkable house.

A Minister, a Senator or a Prince could come here, give his name as Mr Toto and if he wished to remain incognito, he never would be anybody else but Mr Toto while he remained there.

A mask to conceal your features was equally respected. A great many persons wore them, especially the ladies. That is why, as I said before, Madame de Portiera had only been seen by two or three privileged persons.

A few widowers and old bachelors like myself allowed their own names to be used because they had nothing to hide; and they never had cause to regret it.

Pauline (we will use her nom de guerre) wanted to see me to request that I would serve as sponsor to a new guest. I accepted at once and to the usual observations concerning the person, she merely said that he was a Russian.

That was all that I wanted to know. Being near supper time, I took leave of the handsome brunette and strolled over to my restaurant in the Boulevard and afterwards dropped into the Cafe Parisian where I met some old friends, and someone being always ready to play backgammon, we were soon deeply engaged in a game.

It lasted until nine o'clock, when after a few minutes walk on the Boulevard, I returned to the Hotel X. The company was numerous although there was no particular reason for it, and I was soon quite at home with the joyous band. It is true that I often gave the signal for the craziest games and this was perhaps the reason for its popularity.

They were waiting for me. Pauline left a corner of the main parlour and came to meet me, followed by an elegantly dressed man, who at first sight attracted my attention.

A perfect blonde, with soft expressive blue eyes, he was my protegé for the evening and I introduced him according to the prescribed rules. He was received at once with boisterous acclamations.

The conversation of the Count, as he was called, had a rare charm that evening, and he spoke our language with great elegance.

In a few words I put him au courant with the few things he did not already know, and he gave me an idea to propose to the assembled party which seemed to me so amusing that I at once communicated it to the party. The ladies then surrounded Count Alexis and tendered him their congratulations.

It was some time since we had an entertainment and we were most grateful to the newcomer for the idea, which was as follows:

The next night there would be a ball and supper in full evening dress, and the ladies were to dress in gentlemen's attire. It was absolutely forbidden, however, for any one to wear trousers. A light gauze was the most that was allowed for the ladies' covering of the lower parts of the body. Everyone was to disguise his or her identity in the most ingenious manner possible and a mask was obligatory.

After arranging the details of the new entertainment, we separated and sat talking in groups and couples, the latter to give themselves up to the pleasure of fingering, almost always followed by a voluptuous coit in a little room next to the parlour.

CHAPTER THREE

The moment arrived at last to cross once more the threshold of the Hotel X—.

All day I had been as impatient as a child who had been promised to be taken to a play. I felt very queerly in my dress coat, with the tails flapping against my bare bottom, while my prick rose and fell as though it suspected that something unusual was going to happen.

How strange that, on entering the parlour, no one called me by name. It was simply due to the fact that I had succeeded in disguising myself better even than I had hoped. How few persons there were present. Heavens, what a beautiful cunt! Who could be the beauty who displayed such beautiful thighs and such a lovely mount of Venus? My soldier-like instrument stood at "Carry Arms!"

Look at the pretty doll of a girl over there, and who is that big fellow who has just passed his hand between her legs and tried to carry her off. By George, he is strongly built! What a prick he has Aha! She kisses him for fear he might let her fall she holds him fast by the prick and takes the liberty of shaking it.

All the organs of creation are in erection! Who could help it!

"Ladies and gentlemen," began a tall, slender woman whose well defined notch made me wish to fuzzle her on the spot, "I have taken the liberty of inviting two intimate friends to this reunion. I thought that as we were all masked and in disguise beyond recognition, there would be no harm in so doing. The ladies will be here at midnight!"

"It is twelve o'clock already," exclaimed a fat man with a broken voice who knelt down before the beauty and kissed her bower of bliss.

She bent over slightly and raising her coat-tails, displayed the most beautiful bottom in the whole world and forced him to kiss it. After this was done, he held her in spite of her struggles and went on kissing and biting gently.

The beauty soon began to enjoy herself immensely and it was an easy matter to induce her to lie down on the carpet and receive a rod long enough to make a monk jealous, into her handsome boudoir.

At this juncture a beauty with luxuriant black hair on her pussy bent over to have a better view of the performance and the "Big Fellow" before mentioned, took advantage of the opportunity and coming behind her, raised her coat and began to rub his stiffener between the dimpled cheeks of her behind.

But the brunette caught him quickly by the tool and pulled him all around the room, much to the amusement of the company. Suddenly she released him and threw herself upon a sofa, with her legs spread wide open. He understood the invitation at once and shoving his arrow between her thighs quite up to the hilt, he placed his hands under her bottom and picking her up, walked with her all about the room as he futtered her softly.

A sigh of pleasure was soon heard as he made with her body the motions she would have made herself. Then he augmented her voluptuous excitement by inserting his finger in the hole of her arse; she wriggled and held him tightly round the neck and in the delirium of pleasure called him all the sweet names imaginable, until he showered her with sperm.

Then he laid her gently on the sofa again and still under the influence of this particular fuzzing, she continued to move her beautiful legs as if in perfect bliss.

Suddenly the door opened and two masked ladies stood on the threshold. Their dresses being only slightly low in the neck, a murmur of disappointment was heard on every side. Being the first to find words to express the general sentiment, I said:

"Ladies, you have made a mistake, you are masked, it is true, but you should have complied with all the regulations of the evening."

"True, sir," replied the smaller of the two, "but you must excuse novices who could not make up their minds to appear in a costume so primitive, yet so civilised."

"There is no excuse for you, ladies!" answered the Big Fellow, "and you are condemned first, to be whipped according to the regulations, then you must submit to a quarter of an hour's sexual connection with whoever is selected for you, and the rest of the evening you must appear in the costume of Mother Eve!"

The two women looked at each other for an instant and appeared undecided.

"Don't be afraid, ladies," I said, "we are all kindly disposed towards you and will do nothing whatever to displease you."

"This is not the reception we expected," answered the smaller one, in an impatient tone.

Before any more could be said, the ladies found themselves between two gentlemen, whose pricks were in a magnificent state of erection; seats were placed as though they were to assist at an entertainment and we were invited to take our places.

The Big Fellow, armed with a birch, prick erect, approached the taller of the two, whose ample form excited my admiration, and began thus:

"Madame, I have been commissioned to administer to you a whipping. It is a great honour which is conferred upon me. I will not insult you by asking you to undress, a long experience on my part facilitating this proceeding which is a most agreeable one."

"Sir, if you are a gentleman, you will not carry out this odious threat," she answered in a low but firm voice.

The Big Fellow whispered something in her ear and it seemed to reassure the beauty by some promise. Then he began to undress her, turning to the audience:

"Ladies and Gentlemen, this waist is in the latest fashion and somewhat difficult to get off but we will succeed finally." Suiting the action to the word, he removed the garment and our beauty appeared in her corset.

Her alabaster bosoms which were heaving with emotion, appeared like two hemispheres. He kissed them ardently, then passing behind her, he untied her skirts and raising the lady in his arms, lifted her out of the mass of clothing which had fallen around her feet, leaving her in her drawers and corset only.

He had no need to recommend that she remain perfectly still; she did not attempt to make a movement. He finally took off her drawers and corset and the contour of an admirably beautiful form was seen through her only remaining garment, a fine cambric chemise. It showed a superb bottom and a pair of magnificent thighs.

Seizing her by the middle of the body, he gently laid her across his knees on her belly and raised her chemise. Between the slightly parted legs could be seen a thick mass of blonde hair. Her white thighs were as smooth as satin and as firm as marble.

"Oh, sir, be quick, I beg of you, or I shall die of shame!" she murmured. For answer, he struck her arse with the switch and she gave a piercing scream. He struck again but she struggled so that he could not hold her alone. Two gentlemen rushed forward, seized her arms, and the Big Fellow struck again. The beauty twisted and turned her bottom in every way in her agony and rage, to avoid the strokes of the switch which still fell upon her.

Her handsome arse was soon covered with red lines and the Big Fellow, considering the punishment sufficient, had an ointment brought him, with which he rubbed the lovely buttocks.

In doing so, however, he found an opportunity of exploring the treasure hidden between her legs and it soon appeared that the beauty had forgotten the whipping as was giving herself up to the pleasure of being rubbed. Her behind rose and fell voluptuously and she was on the point of "coming" when the Big Fellow asked:

"Who is the happy man who is going to enjoy connection with this lady?"

I was selected by common consent and presented myself before the altar of love, ready to enter from behind. Requesting two gentlemen to hold her slightly raised, when I was about to enter her, she murmured:

"Quick, I beg of you, I am burning with desire!"

With my prick in one hand, while with the other I felt my way, I introduced myself into her warm garden, while she returned the attack with a vigorous movement of her soft white buttocks.

With what ardour she goes on, what happiness it is to me to feel my prick in that region filled with voluptuous moisture. From time to time she squeezes her thighs together, as though to extract the juice quicker from my balls.

The movements of her bottom follow each other with great rapidity and my beauty seems to wish me to penetrate into unknown depths. I am about to attain the supreme point of bliss, when she gives a little cry of voluptuous satisfaction, as she spends with me.

I remain a moment longer with my prick in the yoni of the beauty and it seems as though a little hammer is tapping right upon the end of my tool, a kind of palpitation of the flesh in the interior of the charming retreat. Finally, I withdraw and several ladies carry the beauty to a sofa to rest.

Now comes the turn of the smaller of the two ladies. They were obliged to hold her while they were whipping their companion. Seeing that it would take too long to undress her, a young man, slender and distingué, tied her hands behind her back and dexterously placed her head between his legs.

His prick must have tickled her neck agreeably but nevertheless she did not cease insulting us. In order to get through more quickly he took her skirts and raised them over her back.

The beauty wears drawers which are very wide open. It is an easy matter to whip her without taking them off. He raises her chemise and her arse appears amidst a cloud of laces, not large but round and dimpled, looking like a lovely peach.

Slap! Slap! The young executioner does not think it necessary to use the switch; he merely gives her a whipping with his hand. No use for her to wriggle, she cannot escape a single stroke. Slap! Slap!

"There, Madame, two more than your friend received, because you have been so naughty!"

It is easy to see throughout his performance that the young man does not try to hurt her much and the victim soon begins to understand the farce, not knowing at first whether to laugh or grow angry, but finally she takes it all in good part and laughs heartily.

As a reward for her better behaviour, the company gives her the privilege of choosing the one who is to perform the second operation.

The clear, piercing eyes beneath her mask go slowly round the room, resting an instant on each of the gentlemen. I feel them lingering upon me with some hesitation. They pass on to my neighbour.

Finally the charmer selects a gentleman who is tucked away in a corner near the mantlepiece to be the happy mortal. He is the only one whose thigh finger is not in erection.

Two ladies rush forward to undress the little lady. She allows them to do so with the best grace possible. They strip her completely; she has the form of a child, how charming!

Her little bosoms are scarcely formed and her thighs are slender but round. She is like a charming doll. The gentleman she has selected comes slowly forward and asks what position she prefers.

"Lie down on your back on this sofa," she answers laughingly, "I will get astride of you and do all the work."

At this moment some one tapped me on the shoulder and as I turn, I see that my neighbour is a lady with abundant, curling, golden hair between her legs.

"Monsieur Dormeuil!" she says.

"Yes!" I answer, not suspecting the trap laid for me.

"Ah, I knew it was you!" and then I recognise Clemence. It is too late to retreat.

"Little Sister Clemence, how charming you are in this costume!" I put my hand under her coattail and over her firm, round bottom, slipping it down to her rose garden and allowing my finger to wander in her silky hair.

"Stop, you naughty pirate! I only wished to introduce you to Monsieur Lorille, the Abbé. It is he who is about to offer up a sacrifice to Venus, but poor man, he is dreadfully tired. He gave it to me seven times already tonight and it was so good!"

"Ah, that is the Abbé! Sure enough, he does seem rather worn out," I remarked, "and the little blonde over there seems to be tiring herself out rubbing his cock without great success."

The Abbé seemed to rally, however, and soon he was stiff enough for the little siren to introduce him into the tiny slit that she opens with her fingers. He is now in and leans forward, first to kiss her red lips, then the pink tips of her bosoms. Ah, how well she works! The little woman rises and falls on his mighty organ with the regularity of an amorous machine, rubbing the Abbé's prick delightfully.

Little cries of pleasure escape from time to time, which thrill me with desire from head to foot. At the moment when he is about to spend, she changed her position so as to make it last longer.

I could wait no longer so I put my prick between her two globes and pressed with my fingers her small child-like bosoms.

Those little titties were very firm and her movements led me to think that very shortly I shall flow into her little arse. At any rate, she is about to spend. Oh, there, one ... two ... her plump bottom rises and descends more quickly, she breathes hard, her hand seizes the Abbé's tool and seems to wish to push it up to the hilt. Then comes a shiver that shakes her whole body. I feel that she spends with me and that the Abbé follows suit.

The little woman is all perspiration, and they hasten to her and wrap her up in a cloak.

I now perceive that the Big Fellow has warmed up little Sister Clemence and from the movements of her bottom, I know she is going to get it for the eighth time. I am astonished to see them come towards me and still more to recognise in the hero of the evening, the Russian Count. I was very much pleased and complimented him upon his success.

"Have you discovered Pauline, Count?" I inquired.

"Certainly. She is the tall brunette who announced the arrival of the two ladies, her friends. There she is, talking with the gentleman who so gracefully performed with the little blonde."

Pauline was superb with her majestic limbs, her beautiful bottom that I had admired so much and her handsome retreat so rosy and adorned with a luxuriant hairy covering.

I could not resist the temptation of going to finger her a little. I come up behind her and press a kiss upon each of the globes of her behind. She turns, but not considering the attack dangerous, continues her conversation with Monsieur Lorille.

Her behind is just at the proper height and the temptation being great, I place my tool in the deep rut very gently while I pass my fingers through the curly hair of her treasure.

There is a little sensitive point between the lips of the "beauty" and every time I touch it she gives a slight start with her arse, which excites me more and more. Now my fingers penetrates between the moist lips and moves about in the interior of her boudoir.

She pays no attention to it at first but little by little her buttocks move slightly, and then the movements become more accentuated as my finger moves quicker. Judging that the propitious moment has arrived, I quickly introduce my lance, but the beauty tries to make me lose my hold. I cling to her bottom and hold it like a vice, and the more she tries to throw me off, the more excited I become.

Finally the Abbé comes to my assistance and

holds her hands as she throws up her backside with a movement like a bucking horse.

"Ah, you want it!" she says wildly. "Then take this!" Then comes a punch from her plump behind. But she does not succeed in dismounting me. At last the friction of my pizzle in her shrubbery begins to excite her and with head thrown forward on the Abbé's shoulder, she exclaims:

"Push harder—harder!"

Her hips rise and fall and she would not let me draw out my cocked rod now for anything in the world. Her lascivious movements are now so exciting that I can hardly maintain myself in position. Excited to the highest pitch I give three or four good shoves and drench her with my sperm at the very moment when she spends herself. When she has recovered, I whisper softly in her ear:

"When will you give me another—your friend Dormeuil!"

She answers, half angrily: "I wanted to keep you waiting six months longer. Now the second will be whenever you like."

I kiss her hand and rejoin the Count who says he has enjoyed the scene immensely. The two little ladies who were whipped are now walking in the parlour entirely naked, their bottoms shaking prettily as they move about.

I take advantage of the situation to smack them both as they pass by. The music for the dancing has been playing for the last half hour and it is really a charming sight to watch those half-nude women pass before my eyes. After the dance comes the supper. I am seated near a brunette whom I do not recognise and I give myself the treat of investigating her beauties with one hand under the table.

She touches my stick from time to time to keep it awake and we drink and eat heartily. A wild gallop terminates the whole performance and as the light of day begins to show itself, we conclude that it is time to put on more presentable costumes. The ladies leave first and I go home to seek a much needed rest.

Jean stuck his head into my room to tell me the time of day but I did not hear him. It was five o'clock in the afternoon, before I got up and began my toilet. Jean does not utter a word. He probably thinks he has a new master.

"Has any one been here?"

"Yes, sir, a tall light haired gentleman who left his card. He has been here three times."

"Where is the card?"

Jean handed it to me; it is the Count's. He writes on the card with a pencil that he will return at six o'clock. Evidently Mademoiselle Hortense will not see me today.

The bell rings and Jean introduces my new friend. He comes to invite me to supper at his country seat. I accept with delight. Before leaving, however, I must go and say goodbye to my neighbour.

"Good morning, neighbour!"

"Say good evening, rather; it is late enough for that," answered Madame Benoit with a severe look.

I was holding the knob and as I closed the door, I heard the murmur: "Old Bachelor!"

CHAPTER FOUR

The Count's carriage is at the door and we are soon on the way to his villa, which is situated near Poissy. It is a pretty, modern, cheerful place with gardens on three sides, the other side sloping gently to the Seine, wooded, with narrow paths through it to the river.

The sun is setting and it is one of those beautiful autumn days that remind one rather of spring than the commencement of winter.

A butler does the honours of the house and if there are any other servants they do not appear.

There is a pretty parlour on the first floor, very richly decorated and furnished with sofas and armchairs and mirrors. I am much surprised at the style of the room, to the great amusement of the Count, who passes his arm through mine and leads me to the dining room.

The table is ready and a stroke of the bell brings the butler, to whom he gives orders for serving our meal.

After an excellent supper I stretched myself out in an armchair and the conversation begins.

The Count, who is a good talker, tells many personal adventures, which are all new and hail from all parts of the world. With a large fortune at his command, he has been able to satisfy every whim, and has travelled through America, Asia and part of Africa.

There is no country in Europe with which he is not perfectly familiar and he speaks several languages fluently; in fact he is a charming fellow.

"I had just been travelling in Switzerland," began the Count in his now familiar and well modulated voice, "and I had enjoyed the trip so much that I was tempted to extend my travels further south. I visited all the principal cities in Italy, and the occasion presenting itself to make the trip from Naples to Marseilles with an English family, I accepted the invitation with pleasure, and we set sail.

"For four days the vessel glided smoothly on the Mediterranean and I was almost sorry at last when we arrived at our destination.

"During the trip I had made the conquest of the younger of the girls, who had proposed the most embarrassing things to me: to elope with her or to marry her on her arrival at Marseilles. I got out of the difficulty by promising to go to Manchester the following season, which of course I was careful not to do.

"After taking leave of the Anderson family and thanking them for their kind invitation to visit them in England, I was taken with a severe attack of spleen and hesitated between following the little Miss—which I thought would be ridiculous—and returning to Moscow.

"I do not know what notion possessed me to visit Algiers, which the French had just conquered, but I took passage on the best steamer of the line which was then beginning to run every fortnight.

"The first meal on board the vessel brought together all the passengers around a long dining table. During the first part of the meal I could not fail to see that my neighbour was doing his best to start a conversation with me, and I would have ignored his overtures longer had it been possible. But giving me a nudge on the arm, he said:

" 'This is excellent roast beef, sir, just what we have at home!'

"I turned, and for the first time saw his features. He had a good natured, big round face—simplicity itself—was about forty years of age, and showed that he belonged to the class of well-to-do merchants.

" 'Yes, sir, an excellent roast,' I answered at last.

" 'You are doubtless going to Algiers on business, like myself,' he continued.

" 'No,' I replied, 'I am going on a pleasure trip.'

" 'On a pleasure trip!' cried the good man in amazement.

" 'Certainly, to see the country, hunt, kill time. I cannot kill anything else.'

" 'You are a Parisian,' said he with the air of a man who thinks that only a Parisian could conceive such an extravagant idea.

" 'No, I am a Russian, from Moscow,' I answered.

" 'And I am from Carpentras,' he returned proudly. 'I am going to Algiers on business and I am taking my wife with me. The poor little thing would not be separated from me, so I took her along. We have only been married for six months,' he added confidentially with another nudge as he laughed his great big laugh.

"I was undecided whether to continue my

conversation with him or to go and take a stroll on the deck, but my companion was a regular sticking plaster.

"Once on deck he talked loud enough to be heard a mile away. I was obliged to listen to the history of his fortune and count it over with him several times.

"His name was Theodore Paillard. At about eleven that evening, we retired to our cabins. My cabin was next to his and before I went to sleep, I heard him relating to his wife a lot of things about me of which I was totally ignorant but which he found in his fertile Southern imagination. I then heard Madame Paillard tell him to stop, that she was sleepy, but he would not be quiet, he wanted it, he said . . . he had not had it for three days.

"She said: 'No, it is not convenient in this little box.' I then heard her scold him. " 'You are too big, Theodore. I assure you that you hurt me. Then you are so heavy, you smother me. Let me put it in myself, you are so awkward. Now go ahead, easy. Oh . . . I don't feel anything. Get it for yourself and be quick about it. Don't pinch me like that, you hurt me, I tell you! How long you are . . . You have been drinking, I am certain.'

"Then all was silent for a moment until Madame Paillard's voice rose once more, but this time in anger.

" 'You are always the same, you satisfy yourself and leave me full of your stuff. You are selfish! I have really only had it once since we are married. Ah, now you are going to sleep and I must get up and wash.'

" 'My dear, I am very tired. I promise you that I will give it to you in the morning,' replied he in a pitiful tone. Then I heard the noise of a syringe. Theodore was snoring like a satiated beast. I dreamed all night of Madame Paillard and when I awoke during the night I got to wondering whether she was pretty, or if she were only passable! One is easily satisfied on board ship.

"Early the next morning I was on deck. I was not alone, however; a young woman was walking up and down, stamping her tiny feet from time to time to warm them.

"When she turned I was literally dazzled. An Andalusian beauty with the delicate features of a Princess. This beautiful lady had a superb skin and large black eyes as soft as velvet; she was, moreover, a blonde. I never saw a more beautiful woman in my life. She passed me, smiling, and apparently wholly ignorant of her beauty, which added to it an irresistible charm. I was stunned, fascinated!

"When she turned to walk back I was still in the same spot. I could not lift my eyes from her. All at once a familiar voice fell disagreeably on my ear. It was that of the man from Carpentras, Paillard, whom I was going to send to the devil, when the beautiful lady suddenly took his arm and said coaxingly:

" 'Theodore, please walk with me, I am so cold.'

"Was this Madame Paillard, then; my head was in a whirl.

" 'Come, Virginia, let me introduce you to my friend from Moscow,' he cried in his big voice.

"One must have been very deaf not to have heard him, and advancing towards the ill-assorted couple, I saluted the young woman in my best possible style.

"She received me most gracefully, and turning to

her husband, reproached him for not giving my name. I presented my card to her and as she found my name hard to pronounce, she said:

" 'I will call you Mr Alexis, if you will allow me.'

"We then all three walked the deck for a while, talking and chatting. Theodore was still looking at my card, trying to make out my name. The breakfast bell was a welcome sound as the sea air had given me a ravenous appetite.

"When Madame Paillard was relieved of her wrap, I perceived a full bust that made her tight dress look tighter still. She was twice as pretty, and many curious thoughts rushed through my brain.

"I could scarcely eat. On the second day I became more intimate with the lady and on the third, as we were nearing the Balearic Islands, the sea became quite rough, so she remained in her berth.

"The exuberant nature of Theodore needed more space and air; he could not live closeted in these cabins, he said.

"He came to me to explain the situation and asked me to go down to reassure his young wife, who was terribly afraid of the rolling and tossing of the ship. Lying on a little sofa in the cabin, she looked lovely in her negligee. She got up to meet me and I could see her firm bosoms, entirely without support, like two soft spheres, shaking with every movement.

"We talked of a thousand different things and little by little our conversation turned on burning grounds. She told me that she had come to marry Mr Paillard who had been so kind to her mother! She said this with a sigh, and I felt a rush of desire go through me.

"I could see under her thin dress, and between that dress and her flesh there was a chemise. Attracted to her by an irresistible force, I drew nearer, and as I did so, I had an intense desire to feel that woman's flesh against my own. I could not tell you what I talked about and very likely she did not hear a word.

"Suddenly we seized one another by the shoulders and our mouths formed one, our lips were glued together, my eyes plunged into her and we drank without reserve of the voluptuous bliss of love, that fiery passion beyond compare. There seemed to be a communicative excitement in the very feel of her bare skin, which intoxicated me.

"We would certainly have been surprised by the husband had it not been for his incorrigible habit of loud talking.

"He found me standing by the door. He had not come to remain, he said, but only wanted to see how Virginia was, and finding that she looked well (I should think she would, under the circumstances) he tapped her on either cheek and forced me to sit down on the edge of the bed. He seemed quite delighted to find me so obliging, the poor man. Pshaw! It was his own fault. Why did he want to take advantage of the gratitude of this poor young girl? She was really to be pitied.

"Once more alone, we did not know how to resume the interrupted conversation. Our eyes, however, spoke for us. I went back to my seat at her side and her hands were soon between mine.

"I pressed her voluptuous bosoms with both my hands and carried the licence so far as to unbutton her dress and kiss them.

"'Virginia,' I said, 'let me kiss those treasures.

Let me admire this skin, so soft and white!' and I held up one bosom which filled both my hands.

"The little pink tip, hidden at first in the flesh of the globes, all at once appeared triumphant, I seized it between my lips, then between my teeth and sucked and bit it. I then sought the vermilion mouth of my beauty; her moist lips were trembling, they seemed to invade mine, and when my tongue entered her mouth, I thought she was going into spasms.

"Her whole body quivered, she was almost delirious. What would you have done in my place, with a tool as stiff as an iron bar in your trousers? I carefully raised her dress and as I supposed, there was only a long linen chemise to defend her virtue.

"The obstacle was soon removed and as her legs were parted, it was an easy task to introduce my prick and penetrate into the grotto of love. It was as narrow as that of a maidenhead. She felt a slight pain when I pressed further in but feeling my stiff prick in her tiny, moss covered bower, she became furiously agitated and seizing me by the neck, would have smothered me between her large bosoms, had I not freed myself.

"To maintain my position in this retreat, I was obliged to pass my hand beneath her bottom and moderate the hysterical leaps she made, due to a desire so long repressed.

"I now slipped my tongue between her teeth and ran my weapon of war up and down along her little furrow. She suddenly seemed to quiet down and enjoy calmly my amorous embraces.

"Nothing could indicate that she had attained the supreme point of bliss when I was about to spurt my provision of sperm into her retreat, except a slight shudder, followed by complete exhaustion.

"I left her undisturbed for a few minutes while I admired her magnificent thighs, her superby body, so round and firm, and her little pussy of hair like that of a child of sixteen. I proceeded then to wash her, remembering the reproaches she had addressed to her husband the night before.

"The contact of the cold water brought her to her senses. She opened her eyes in astonishment, until she remembered all, and then, jumping down, she threw her arms around my neck and pressed her lips passionately to mine.

"The same scene was renewed the following day amid long talks. She regretted the separation which must come at our landing and it also worried me, for I really hungered after the woman, I had not possessed her enough. I promised to accompany her everywhere but when she thought of how she would be obliged to submit to her husband whom she did not love, burning tears would roll down her cheeks. I was kissing them away gently one day when an idea struck me, and I resolved to communicate it to her and convince her of the success of my scheme whereby we would not be separated on landing.

"I communicated to Virginia my idea whereby we could continue our relationship but she refused to listen at first. The more she refused, the more feasible it seemed to me and I insisted. At last she laughed heartily and was ready to put it into execution. I explained the intrigue to her in every detail.

"Soon after our arrival she was to appear unhappy. Theodore was to find her always gloomy and two days before the departure of the steamer she was to propose returning to France.

"He, stingy, and going to Algiers for the purpose of making money, would not think of consenting to go back with her, and would not allow her to return alone. I would advise him to let her go alone, and the journey being short, the Captain and stewardess would take good care of her.

"By degrees he would become accustomed to the idea, then I would whisper in his ear that without his wife, he could take advantage of the innumerable chances which were never wanting here. Ah, if he should only find a Moorish beauty! One of those ideal women which exist in novels at home, but which are here in flesh and blood.

"I was certain of the success of the scheme. She was to go on board of the steamer, excuse herself a few minutes and go into a cabin where she would find a Moorish costume which I would provide for her. When the first bell rang for the departure, she was to go back on land and leave the rest to me.

"'But you see, Alexis, the thing is impossible! When I go on land I will find my husband with you. He will accost me and then what language will I speak? I only speak French as it is, and no other language but this and Spanish.'

"This remark disconcerted me for a moment but I soon found a solution. At a pinch we might speak French; there would be nothing extraordinary in a Moorish woman speaking French, but we would have less liberty. He might recognise the voice and a familiar expression might spoil the whole game.

"However, I remembered that when at college in France, the pupils had a way of conversing by adding a termination to each monosyllable, article, etc., being careful to make it accord in sound with the words used. You finally got an outlandish jargon, which no one could understand who did not possess the key.

"Madame Paillard was quite sure that her husband, who was somewhat of a simpleton anyway, would not understand such a language. So everything was settled.

"The young woman, in ten minutes understood the whole system and I left her, recommending that she practise speaking in this manner when alone, feeling that in two or three days she would speak it with facility.

"A few days after our arrival in Algiers, according to programme, Madame Paillard became very gloomy; her husband seemed quite uneasy and one day when I told her that a steamer sailed within forty-eight hours, she declared to Theodore that she wanted to return to France. She was dying with ennui, she said.

"Everything happened as we had foreseen. I became really eloquent in the cause and Paillard decided to let her return alone. I arranged everything with the Captain and Stewardess. Madame Paillard's trunks were to remain in Marseilles until further orders.

"We accompanied her to the steamer and at the last moment, the husband would go with her, but the magic words 'Moorish Beauty,' whispered in his ear, decided him to remain. The young woman excused herself and disappeared down the companion way, smothering her laughter.

"At the first signal for departure, Theodore wished to rush down and kiss her once more good-bye but at that instant a woman, heavily veiled,

226

showing her two handsome eyes, passed by as light as a butterfly and brushing by our friend on the way, she gave him a burning glance.

" 'There is a Moorish woman!' I said hurriedly, 'come do not let us lose this chance, it is a rare one, I assure you.'

"He instantly forgot wife and all, and trotted breathlessly after the woman who was walking a few steps ahead of him. He overtook the beauty and was talking to her when I joined them but, of course, she did not understand a word of French. 'She does not understand French, Mr Alexis,' said he in such pitiful tones that I could not help bursting out laughing.

" 'Do not distress yourself,' I said, 'I understand her language and will talk to her,' and there I was, chattering away with the Moorish woman in the language I had taught her in ten minutes.

"I was obliged to translate M. Paillard's propositions, which were businesslike, and I made him understand that being in a foreign country, under no consideration whatever to attempt to raise the woman's veil for that meant instant death.

"He promised faithfully not to try the experiment and I felt no more uneasiness on that score.

"I had rented a little villa about five minutes walk from the city, surrounded by beautiful gardens. I explained once more to Mr Paillard that Moorish women never uncovered their faces; that they always eat and dress alone. To seek to uncover their face is a crime. He was easily convinced.

" 'Do you think I could sleep with her?' he asked eagerly.

" 'Certainly! Nothing easier!' I answered. 'You will certainly succeed on that point.'

"Everything passed without mishap. I talked all day to the young woman (Madame Paillard), and when it was time to retire at night, she hung on my arm and gave Theodore to understand that she would prefer spending the first night at least with me.

"Theodore retired to the room next to ours and was soon snoring the snore of the just. Left alone, I seized the young woman in my arms.

"She was lovcly in her somewhat original costume. I helped her to undress and for fear of a surprise, we concluded she had best sleep with the veil.

"The night was warm and I persuaded her to sleep naked. I felt a foolish desire to view her charms, and took off ther chemise in spite of her remonstrances.

"She was a mixture of strength and weakness; her neck was slender and I have already spoken of her handsome bosom. Her luxuriant bottom was enough to make the Colonel of the Tenth Cuirass-iers jealous, as they say in Russia.

"I did not know what to handle first; I went from her cunt to these two beautiful globes, which stood out as firm as marble. I felt like eating her up and when I put my face between her admirable thighs, she held my head tight enough to smash it.

"I took her beautiful body in my arms and laid her on the bed; then, placing myself over her, I began to explore her sweet little cunny with my tongue. My prick was placed just above her face and in her excitement she took hold of it and rolled it with her hands. My tongue was shooting a thou-sand strokes into her vagina and she would lift up her body in her passion, then give a sudden pressure of her legs on my head which nearly sent me wild.

"The very tip of my prick was burning with ardent fire. I put it into her mouth. Oh, how she sucked it! Her tongue gave me an indescribable sensation; my ardour became double and I sucked and bit the lips of her little cunny in a perfect storm of passion.

"Feeling that I was about to spend in her mouth, I withdrew my prick and pushed it between her beautiful bosoms, telling her to press them against my prick as I tickled her two little strawberries.

"This sensation, added to the sensuous lingering of my tongue in her voluptuous vulva, soon threw her into the wildest spasms of delight, and with true cries of delirious joy, she inundated my tongue with her delightful fluid.

"Her cries had awakened Theodore and suddenly I heard him jump from his bed to the floor.

"I had neglected to lock the door and he walked in without further ceremony. Fortunately the light was out and we had time to prepare ourselves. He said his prick was in such a state of erection that he absolutely must have the Moorish woman. What was to be done?

"She did not want him in the least, and he was bound to be satisfied. I made him believe that it was bad form to enter into the vagina of a Moorish woman at the first meeting and that he must content himself with rubbing his prick between the cheeks of her bottom; that she would agree to it, I guaranteed.

"He was so excited that his teeth chattered and he agreed to accept anything that we proposed.

" 'Tell him to make haste,' said the young woman.

" 'You must move your arse so as to hasten matters,' I suggested.

" 'I will,' answered the poor boob.

"He was soon astride her bottom and placing his immense prick between the two hillocks, he began to rub and she to wriggle. Sometimes she raised herself and rubbed her behind against his prick so that he touched her cunt.

" 'It is strange but this backside reminds me of my wife's,' he would say almost out of breath.

" 'Do not talk that way!' I said boldly.

"He soon began puffing like a porpoise and lay down on the young woman's bottom.

"She complained that he was smothering her and I was obliged to raise him up and tell him to be more lively in his movements. She rubbed him a little while longer and when finally a jet of sperm inundated her back, she gave a sigh of relief, which caused him to ask her if she had spent.

" 'Oh, yes, yes,' she replied, and he went away quite satisfied to resume his snoring. I washed her, poor little thing, and fatigued with such hard work, she fell asleep.

"Ever after that I locked the door carefully.

"This went on for a month and only once during that time was he allowed to even rub his cock between the buttocks of his wife. He was far from suspecting her of being his own wife and everything went well with one exception.

"Then it happened in broad daylight when he could not possibly contain himself any longer. I unfastened the full, Turkish trousers of the beauty and held her head between my legs. She took advantage of this to suck me gently while her husband agitated his prick between the cheeks of her bottom.

"This time it rather amused her. She did not pretend to help him and he kept asking me to tell her to move her arse more. He had to spend, however, and I advised him to catch the sperm in his handkerchief. I did not care to receive the charge.

"To tell you of the delightful nights I spent with that lovely woman during that month would take me a very long time and become monotonous, so I will end by saying that all went well.

"It did not surprise Paillard that I should take the beautiful woman to France with me. On arriving at Marseilles, I pretended to leave her at the Hotel until she could be dressed as other women dress in Europe, and she started at once for Carpentras; her mother was to say that she had spent a month with her and everything would be settled all right.

"I parted with her reluctantly but she promised to see me again some day. I detained her husband a day in Marseilles in order to give her time to have everything settled.

"Thus ends my story.

"Ah, you want a conclusion; well, here it it!

"After leaving the husband at the station, I started for Paris where I remained some months as as I was about to leave the city, I received a letter from Theodore, announcing the birth of a boy whom he had named Alexis, with the full consent of his wife.

"Dear old Paillard—this act of courtesy was really due to me."

The Count had been very animated as he related this adventure, but now he became grave and melancholy and seemed pensive, shaking his head as though to cast off some thought.

"My dear friend, thrown as I have been for the past fifteen years amid pleasure, with no time to study the exact moment for my conquest, I have certainly committed acts which sober people might call indelicate.

"If indeed I have sometimes gone too far in my mad career, if I have brought grief to some hearts and pain to some young slits, at least once in my life I have had scruples.

"Let me confide this strange adventure to you; it will be a relief to me. You have made a study of mankind and I feel certain that you will not laugh at me but will understand my feelings in the matter."

CHAPTER FIVE

"Three years ago, and about eighteen months before my trip to Algiers, I was on my estate, a few miles from Moscow. The winter was very severe and I went to the city as seldom as possible, even when it was a question of sensual satisfaction. Aside from one or two large landowners like myself, I saw no one, and spent the time looking after my servants, hunting wolves and reading a few erotic books, which were not calculated to calm my passions.

"I soon noticed the daughter of one of my farmers, a handsome girl, and the only one who appeared to be modest among all the girls and women with whom I was thrown in contact night and day.

"It was a rare thing to see her smile, but when she did, she showed beautiful teeth, and two dimples would make two deep holes in her rosy cheeks.

"She had luxuriant hair, as black as jet, which she wore in a braid that hung far below her waist; the short dress, which came just below her knees, displayed two handsome legs, round and firm, while her large black eyes were shaded by heavy lashes. She was beautiful, very beautiful, and just sixteen.

"As she was extremely modest, I did not know how to make propositions to her which many of the others would have quickly accepted. Several times I tried to enter into conversation with her. I questioned her first about her parents in a careless, indifferent manner, then I laughingly asked her if she had a betrothed. She looked at me quietly, surprised perhaps at such a question, but she did not answer.

"For a whole month I remained in this embarrassing position. Sometimes I would wake up at night after dreaming that I had her in bed with me, that I had fully possessed her, and I would turn over and find myself alone with my prick at full stand. I would then make up my mind to fly from the spot that very day or force her to surrender, but the day would pass just as the preceding one and nothing came of it.

"Sometimes I surprised her looking at me, but the look was so frank, so innocent, that I did not dare to speak.

"I do not know how or why, but her mother perceived what was going on, and coming to me with tears in her eyes, told me the farm did not produce enough to support the family. Praising her modest daughter, she begged me to take her into my service. I was delighted with the proposition but was careful not to show it, and dismissed the woman without making any promises.

"A few days later I had a visit from the father and finally I consented to take the young girl.

"One day, a theft having been committed in the house, all the accusations fell upon the young girl and I had her summoned before me in order to question her myself.

"She scarcely deigned to defend herself. She had not stolen anything and suspected no one of the deed. This was all she would say. At the head of the female department of the household I had a dragon of a woman who was extremely strict and whose devotion to me was, without question, devout. She advised me to have the girl whipped to make her confess the crime. I was obliged to consent and ordered the whipping to be administered in my presence.

"The girl looked on calmly while the preparations were made for the torture, but what amazed me was to see her quietly undress herself, throwing to the floor one by one her articles of clothing until she was naked to the waist.

"Her back was turned to me. Ah, when the woman struck her on the back with the strap, I almost cried out, and ordered her to stop and retire.

"I got up, took the young girl in my arms and gently drew her on my knees as I tried to reassure her—it was only then that she burst into tears. I tried to draw her hands away from her face, which she had hidden in them; I wanted to see her bewitching eyes bathed in tears.

"She was so beautiful thus that I lost my head, threw her brutally on the sofa and rushed upon her like a hungry wolf.

"I kissed her tiny bosoms furiously. They were firm as marble. I stuck my head between her legs and there was the peculiar perfume of a clean woman which made me delirious with lubric passion.

"Like an animal, I squeezed the firm, rosy lips of her hidden parts and rubbed my face against them. I was intoxicated by the delicious odour. I stuck my tongue between the lips of her little pussy. I drew out and licked it like an amorous animal, for I too, was an animal then in my sensuous desire.

"Suddenly surprised at not feeling her move, I disengaged my head from her skirts and was not a little bewildered to find her sobbing as though her heart would break.

"I took both her hands in mine and placed my fiery lips upon hers. The tears streamed down her cheeks and dropped one by one on my breast. Her mouth seemed insensible to my caresses.

"Finally calmed by the sight of so much grief, I suddenly awoke as from some horrible nightmare, picked up her clothing and covered her nakedness. This seemed to calm her somewhat and when my paroxysm was over I got her to talk.

"She swore on the image of the Holy Virgin that she was innocent and she gently reproached me for my conduct. It had hurt her so much that she began sobbing again.

"I was ashamed of myself and begged her pardon. I felt vile, degraded before this pure young girl and promised not to annoy her any more. After talking about half an hour, I sent her back, consoled now, to her occupation, and told the other servants that I was convinced of her innocence and would not allow anyone to be wanting in respect to her.

"I was not myself for several days after this incident. I dreaded to meet the young girl and took a thousand precautions to avoid her, and yet I was happy in knowing that she was in the house.

"Naturally, we often came in contact and she met me with the same beautiful smile. I felt the passion which I had for her growing stronger and stronger and it was then that I determined to leave Moscow and go to St Petersburg.

"I attended all the society balls, and one night as I was helping the Viscountess Xenia on with her furs, she invited me to accompany her home. I sent away my sleigh and slipped into hers.

"Leaning against each other during the ride, I responded to the coquetries of the beautiful woman as best I could. When we arrived at the house, she invited me to come in, which I did with pleasure, not suspecting for a moment that I was to possess that very night the most sought after woman in St Petersburg.

"I was shown into an immense, well-lighted parlour and requested to wait a few moments. I stretched myself in an armchair and was thinking of nothing in particular, when a servant informed me that he had been ordered to take me to Madame's apartments. I followed him and we soon reached a sort of boudoir, hung in white satin, with sofas and chairs to match, and a huge mirror.

"Words cannot describe the comfort and elegance of the room. The mistress of the house soon entered, wrapped in a black silk dressing gown without any trimming; the garment became her complexion admirably. She invited me to sit down on the sofa beside her. She wore little golden yellow slippers, with black silk stockings, embroidered with yellow and was tapping the floor with her tiny feet, and continuing the coquetry begun in the sleigh.

" 'They tell me many curious things about you, Count' . . . she began.

" 'What do they say, Madame?'

" 'Oh, they say that you are a fast man, for one thing.'

" 'Where is the man who has not had that said of him?'

" 'True, but there are some little scandals here and there. In Vienna, Paris, etc., with ladies of good society.'

" 'It is proof then, Madame, that I have succeeded in finding favour everywhere except in St Petersburg. As yet I have not had that good fortune here.'

" 'You are so seldom here,' she said, pouting.

" 'It rests with you alone, whether I stay or not!' I whispered, taking her hand.

" 'Really, sir?' she responded with a look that was a challenge.

"I seized her round the waist and tried to kiss her and during the struggle somehow or other, the dressing gown suddenly became unfastened and flew open from top to bottom, displaying her goddess-like form entirely naked.

"It was only an apparition, however, as she rushed out of the door and closed it after her. Then she made me the most delightful promises if I would undress and put on the costume she would hand me through the door.

"I had long been accustomed to any proposition, however strange it might be, so I took care not to refuse. I waited, and in a few moments, the door was slightly opened and a lot of clothing fell at my feet.

"At first I had some trouble in making out what I had picked up from the floor, but at last I found that it was a very pretty wrapper, handsomely trimmed with red lace, and a pair of woman's drawers and stockings long enough to reach to my thighs.

" 'Are you ready?' asked the Countess impatiently.

" 'Not yet, Madame, but I will be presently.' I replied.

"I had got into the drawers and stockings when

she entered quickly. I thought it was a saucy little boy who stood before me and the sudden erection of my member betrayed the emotion produced upon me by the lascivious costume of the charmer.

"She had on black velvet breeches fitting her superb figure tightly, little socks reached just above the ankles and her tiny feet were encased in black velvet slippers. The upper part of her body was clothed in a fine shirt, puffed round the waist, a short jacket reaching to the middle of her back, while a broad lace collar covered her shoulders. Added to that, were blonde curls falling in ringlets around her neck.

"I rushed forward to seize her, wishing to add the sensual pleasure of touch to that of looking at her but she stopped me with an angry gesture and offered to assist me in getting into the wrapper. She passed her hands several times over my cock on purpose and I took those occasions to steal a kiss 'on the fly.' I was soon dressed and she commanded me to sit down in an armchair and listen to her with undivided attention.

" 'You are going to have a very bad opinion of me, Count, But if I have determined to indulge in this caprice, it is because I have heard your discretion praised as much as your gallant adventures, and I feel very certain that you will banish this evening's experience from your memory entirely.'

" 'I will forget it for everyone else, but I can never forget it for you, Madame,' I replied.

" 'That is quite sufficient, sir, and now let us abandon ourselves entirely to pleasure . . . come!'

"She now dragged me along a little passage which led to a chamber below. I will not attempt to describe the luxury of this room. She disappeared in a secret closet and brought out an enormous dildo. I was then obliged to play the lady and she made all the advances and caressed me in every possible manner. She slipped her hand under my wrapper and petted my bottom; she kissed me, but would not allow me to touch her. However, she told me to whip her if she behaved badly and as her big bottom was very tempting in her velvet trousers, I contented myself with giving her slaps on top of her trousers to begin with.

"Her manners became worse and worse, however, so that at last I threw her across my knees, hastily unbuttoned her trousers and gave her a great whipping. Her beautiful buttocks were so fat that in passing my hand over them, near the thighs, the whole compactness moved into a solid block but she held her legs so tightly closed that it was impossible to take the liberty of touching all the beauties which were in that near vicinity.

"After a goodly number of well applied smacks, the beautiful bottom became quite red, and no doubt considering that to be sufficient, she ran away, but her face expressed more passion than before, and returning to me, she raised my wrapper to my waist and fingered my cock for a moment.

"Then laying her head on the edge of the bed, she gave me a cat-like invitation by presenting her handsome behind to me. I rubbed my now thoroughly stiffened member between the beautiful cheeks of her bottom. Then she seized my hand, but would not allow me to put it anywhere near her secret parts.

" 'Not yet,' she said, 'be patient,' and she rubbed her backside against my appendage. A momen later she let my hand go so as to pass her hands slyly under my balls.

"She finally used her handsome behind so well, that I spent at the moment she was fingering me 'a little all over,' as she called it, to accelerate the matter. Then, turning round, she saw my instrument hanging down. She gave me a malicious look and going after the big dildo, she tied it round my waist. She then used a little ointment on it, and presenting to me her superb doorway, whose proportions I was obliged to admire, asked me to introduce the big thing into it.

"I thought that would be impossible, but she wriggled and pressed against me until she got it almost all the way in. This performance took place on the edge of the bed; she unbuttoned her waist and I could see her alabaster bosoms, white, firm, well developed and nicely separated. I gently rubbed her handsome slit with the enormous tool and she seemed absolutely delirious with pleasure.

" 'Open the valve when I tell you,' she murmured, as she continued to play upon it. She had with a sudden movement wound her legs around my waist and seemed to wish to push the dildo up to the handle.

"I never saw so much passion in my life. With her eyes half closed, she seemed to be lost in another world. I stooped over her, squeezed her bosoms which appeared to excite her still more, and finally, as if in agony, she cried out:

" 'Let the valve go—let it go!'

"I did so, and a copious flow of tepid fluid inundated her handsome cunt. She was still slowly heaving and enjoying this internal 'coit' as I continued the frigging movements with the enormous dildo. Little by little she became more excited and it seemed to me that my pizzle attained the proportions of the big dildo itself. I then slowly untied it and making believe it had slipped out by accident, I introduced my instrument into her loins.

"Her cunt was large but full of voluptuousness and as I shoved my wedge in, I kissed her delicious bosoms, her neck, her belly and then her lascivious mouth.

"She sustained this second assault admirably well and it lasted long. When she cried out again to let the valve go, I was on hand with a new supply of sperm which appeared to satisfy her.

"She remained unconscious for a few moments, then got up, her face crimson, and her body exhausted. I advised sleep and she answered with a smile that indeed she thought she needed it.

"I dressed myself and took leave of the beautiful Countess after taking a voluptuous kiss from her moist coral lips.

"She offered me her sleigh for my return but as my house was not very far off, I preferred to walk there.

"Two days after this I was awakened by a terrible noise at the door of my room. My servant answered the bell and returned to say that a young girl had introduced herself into the house and refused to leave without speaking to me. I ordered that she come down and to my astonishment, I saw, once more, my little servant girl.

"She looked like a beggar and her garments were in shreds. She finally told me that after my departure she had been so unhappy that she determined to follow me. A little money allowed her to travel in a sleigh part of the way, then her purse being empty, she was obliged to walk the rest of the journey.

"The tortures of all kinds she must have suffered gave me an idea of the strength of her will. The poor little thing acknowledged that she loved me and that she would surely kill herself it I abandoned her. I felt an emotion which was entirely new to me. It was impossible to place her with the other servants and the only thing I could do was to persuade her to go to France with me, where I could put her in a school for a few years.

"Three years have elapsed now and I have had occasion to appreciate the progress which my protégé has made in every possible way, in learning and in accomplishments of all kinds.

"When my thoughts turn to her it is like balm to my heart. However, she could not remain in school any longer. The Superintendent wrote me lately that she had nothing more to teach her and a few days ago I gave orders to have her brought here, where she is at present.

"I have had two interviews with Wanda—that is the name I have given her—and her love for me is so intense that I dread to see her. When I propose to find a husband for her, she goes into hysterics and I had to promise to make no more allusions to her marriage.

"Such is my position, M. Dormeuil, what would you do in my place?"

"I really cannot say, my dear Count. It is most embarrassing. You cannot marry her and you do not wish to make her your mistress."

He seemed for a time lost in a profound reverie and did not reply for a few moments.

"She wishes to see me this evening and I am

afraid I may weaken," he said at last. "Let me conduct you, dear friend, to a closet, near her room and if passion should get the best of me, come to my assistance, I pray you."

The greater part of the evening was already spent and we had to hasten our visit to Wanda before she should retire. The Count preceded me and made me enter a closet next to the room, at the door of which he knocked.

"Who is there?" called a fresh young voice.

"It is I, Alexis."

"Ah, at last," She cried, and I heard her run to the door. "How glad I am to see you, I feared you would forget my request."

"You see, do you not, that I have not forgotten it, since I am here."

There was a little hole in the door of my hiding place which seemed to have been made on purpose. I peeped through it and saw her on her knees before him. She implored him to keep her with him; she would be his slave.

She is as handsome as the Count has described her, but taller and more distinguished looking in her white wrapper. As she holds his hands and kisses his face, her expression denotes sincere love. She pulls him towards a large armchair and innocently sits on his knees, as she would have done with her father when a child; while with all the grace imaginable, she tries to extract a promise from him that he will not leave her.

It was too much for my Russian friend to withstand and naturally he seized her head and covered her face with kisses. They are entwined in each other's arms. Their bodies are like one. It would have seemed a crime to me to disturb them, notwithstanding the request made by the Count.

How she twists herself like a snake; now they have fallen pell-mell on a beautiful white bearskin on the floor, and he passes one leg between her naked thighs, and she, following her natural instinct, rubs herself against him.

I could not blame him. As I looked at them, I felt my own prick stiffen up like a poker. When he placed his instrument between her beautiful thighs, I thought he only did his duty, for she was breathlessly wishing for it.

The jerks of the young girl's body became less marked, and all at once she gave a cry of pain! It was only transitory, however, for she entwined herself round the Count more closely than ever. She literally covered his face with kisses and laughed and cried in the same breath.

It is impossible for me to see her body with the exception of her thighs which escape her drawers, but that is enough to convince me of the beauty of the rest.

She must have spent several times, although she does not wish to let him go. She has turned over on her side and shows me her back. Her drawers are slightly open and as she pushes with her bottom, I can see her crack with the Count's lance-like prick imbedded in it.

Her backside must be enormous, for it almost splits the delicate envelope that confines it.

The Count has just spent but she still remains sticking to him and does not allow her mouth to leave his for an instant.

I judged that the amorous combat was at an end and in order not to receive any reproaches from the

Count, I pretended to be asleep. When he shook me, I begged his pardon for having fallen asleep. He excused me politely and conducted me back to his room without saying a word about Wanda. The next morning the Count came to wake me himself and had been thoughtful enough to have my breakfast brought to me in bed.

I rose and he conducted me to his bath. We talked of a thousand and one things and his conversation was very animated; he seemed much happier and livelier than was his wont.

"Come," said he, "I am going to show you my library."

He led the way to a room whose style was most severe. but where all the erotic works of French, English and Spanish authors were arranged on shelves.

While I admired the handsome collection, the Count pressed a spring and a little drawer flew open which contained some volumes carefully wrapped in silk. He took them from their hiding place with the greatest care and handed them to me one by one. I read their titles:

   A Youthful Adventurer
   The Comtessa Marga
   The Perfumed Garden
   Venus in India
   Adventures Of Lais Lovecock
   A Spanish Gallant
   Memories of a Voluptuary

and numerous other works of a similar character.
The British Museum contains some of these

works, which are not only very rare but also master-pieces of erotic literature.

The collector who could obtain any of them would be fortunate and find their perusal most entertaining. They rank high in their line, and will make many a one stand.

"I must absent myself for some hours," he continued, "but you can spend your time here pleasantly and read anything you like."

As soon as he left, I began to read the rarest of these works. The rest were already know to me, at least those in English and French. *The Horn Book* is a remarkable work and also *The Open Chamber*.

When he returned it seemed to me as if he had only been gone a few moments, so much was I interested in my reading. He announced that he had prepared everything for an agreeable evening, but he would not tell me anything more. He expressed his regrets at not being able to spend the rest of the day with me and added that he had to go out and make a few calls.

I had forgotten Paris, Madame Benoit, Madame Cuchond and the rest! I must go too, or they would send out a general alarm. The Count held me back, smiling, and assured me that everything would be all right, as he would go himself to see Madame Benoit and the others and explain everything.

I preferred it so and agreed to remain. I resumed my erotic reading which caused the remainder of the day to pass very quickly. When five o'clock struck and it began to get dark, I had devoured a large part of the contents of the secret drawer.

The Count returned a little before six o'clock and soon we partook of an excellent supper.

After supper—we took our supper in the

parlour—I perceived that my friend was in the best of humours. He had been to Madame X—, had seen Pauline, Clemence, the Abbé, and a few others. They did not know what to think of my absence; he had given them some kind of an explanation and they were convinced that I had gone on a hunting expedition some miles away.

The parlour, I now perceived, had been robbed of its furniture, and there was an open space in the middle of the room. The Count invited me to be seated on a sort of ottoman, low but delightfully comfortable, while he on another, just opposite to mine.

The atmosphere is perfumed, while the light is so arranged as to be of every imaginable colour. I feel that my friend is reserving a surprise for me. What can it be?

In answer to his call, Ivan, his faithful servant, brings in two Turkish pipes with their long stems. I would have preferred a good cigar, but for the novelty of the thing I accept the pipe.

We are sitting quietly, when the curtain over the door moves and a woman or girl with a musical instrument enters the room. I say woman or girl, for she is so wrapped up that I cannot see her face. The Count smokes on without manifesting either surprise or curiosity, and I do the same.

The woman begins the entertainment, and sits down on a cushion and commences to play a lazy, monotonous air. Two other women enter the room at this juncture and their dance, monotonous at first, becomes more animated as the music becomes faster.

They turn round each other in the middle of the room and all at once appear to me as if enveloped

248

in a coil of tulle. Sure enough, they have loosened their muslin robes and as they dance, they unwind them. I can distinctly see their legs through their thin single skirt. The dance becomes more and more exciting; the two girls soon become entwined in each other's arms and seem intoxicated.

Suddenly they tear off their veils and I can see their forms which are admirably moulded. Both are brunettes and apparently sixteen or seventeen years of age. They each wear a small jacket, open in front from the middle of the body to the cunt, while a many-coloured belt, encircles their waists. Besides this, the only garment for each is a gauze skirt.

They must, however, have something else for an undergarment, for it is impossible to see their flesh clearly. They embrace and, still retaining their steps, kiss each other feverishly. Each in turn passes her head beneath the other's jacket and kisses the snowy white bosom beneath.

They soon unfasten their short skirts and throw off their belts. They are bewitching in their unique costumes, a little waist reaching scarcely down to the hips and a light yellow scarf covering their bottoms and hidden places, now complete their outfits.

They continue to excite one another, and the music seems to make them frantic with passion. Hastily they snatch off their clothing and now contemplate each other in almost total nudity.

They roll on the floor like playful kittens, their fingers tickling each other's private parts, while little amorous cries escape their lips. They handle each other's bosoms and tongue their lips. The youngest seems to be the most excited and while she kisses her companion, she puts her tongue far into her mouth; her bottom moves like lightening and when her companion touches her with her fingers between her legs, she starts as though it actually burned her.

She wishes to be played with and yet seems to evade the touch. She jumps astride her friend's bottom and rubs her little cunt on her, and while she fingers her pussy, the other turns her head to receive a kiss, and the music plays on.

At last they have reached the desired degree of excitement and each now feverishly places the head of the other between her own legs, while they caress each other with rapid strokes of their tongues.

The tallest one has her back towards me, and shows me her arse with its little pink hole. Beneath her I see the tongue and lips of the youngest. The little hole seems to open and close as the enjoyment becomes greater. The one underneath her sustains her, and her beautiful bottom looks like a split hemisphere in pink satin.

I never witnessed a more exciting scene, and my prick, as a proof of my feelings, is swollen to its utmost. The Count is still passive. The two young girls are about to spend and their bodies are quivering with passion. The beautiful behind which fascinates me, rises and falls, opens and closes with marvellous rapidity.

Suddenly they both spend and the smaller seems actually to want to eat the little cunny which she has between her teeth. She bites it in her amorous delirium.

My prick makes a movement at the very moment that the girls spend and I have just time to introduce my handkerchief into my breeches to receive the discharge.

They are still stretched upon the floor to recuperate their strength, and their beautiful bodies give a voluptuous tremor from time to time. I turn my head towards the Count and when I look for the erotic pair, they have disappeared.

My friend's eyes are a little more brilliant than usual but that is all. The servant enters with two dressing gowns and the Count invites me to lay aside my ordinary clothes, and sets the example.

He now gave an order in Russian and Ivan entered with a tray and two glasses and a little flask containing a bright red liquid. Two little pieces of fruit, nicely cut, accompanied the liquid. I was served first and put the fruit into my mouth after seeing the Count do so.

"When you feel a little hard substance," he said, "swallow it without uneasiness. It is a preparation which invigorates you."

I had just come to a sweet substance and according to instructions, swallowed it. Ivan presented me then with the glass of liquor which I drank. The liquid seemed to instil new life in me; I felt its warmth pervade my whole being. I had not before noticed a large handsome woman standing before me. She wore Turkish trousers of black silk, while between her thighs was a large mass of silky hair. She holds an enormous dildo in her hands and her bare bosoms, large, well separated, and as firm as marble spheres, seem to shiver in voluptuous anticipation.

At this moment she smiles at the Count and seats herself astride of a chair, after tying the dildo to one of her heels. She now introduces it into the lips of her cunt, while with a movement of her legs she puts it in rapid motion.

It soon appears that she enjoys this game immensely, when suddenly, not finding her legs agile enough, she unties the dildo and throwing herself on the floor, spreads her legs wide apart and shakes the enormous affair about inside of her.

In her passion she throws herself first upon her belly, then on her side, sometimes working fast, then again slowly, very slowly. Sometimes she holds it motionless and with the movement of her arse, presses it in; then again she places it upright on the floor and after letting her trousers down around her feet, she steps over it and forces her cunt open with its large end. Her great round arse rises and falls like a voluptuous machine, as she pushes it up to the hilt.

Her buttocks rebound faster and faster, and finally she throws herself upon her back and reaches the last great paroxysm of enjoyment by gently rubbing with her cunt, as she squeezes the dildo between her powerful thighs, which seem to be made of stone.

Thus, almost nude as she was, she resembled an antique statue and as she displayed her magnificent treasures, my prick fairly ached to take the place of the dildo which she was moving gently in her palpitating organ.

A slight sign from the Count aroused her and she retired slowly, her enormous arse, between whose cheeks I would willingly have disported myself, shaking as she walked away.

CHAPTER SIX

The Count suddenly began laughing; I felt the same desire, gradually creeping over me. I laughed and kept on laughing, unable to stop.

Lights seem to flash before my eyes, but I imagine some one is tying me; a bright light approaches me suddenly. I am in a delightful garden. It is immense—it seems to be a conservatory.

Delicious music is heard, first in the distance, then nearer. The scene changes like a flash. I am now in a room all hung in black; the music changes, a lovely woman enters and undresses herself. The scene is familiar to me. I have seen it somewhere. I finally recognise it as a scene in the passage of a book entitled *The Exposition*, which I have been reading. After having enjoyed reading it, I have the pleasure of seeing it. Then all is dark again, until another flash of light illuminates the next scene.

Two brigands have seized a magnificent woman; she begs for mercy and offers them money but I can see in their eyes that they will only be satisfied by assaulting the beauty. One of them is a strapping big fellow, but handsome withal; he cuts the laces of her bodice with a single stroke and begins to feel her bosoms. She struggles vainly, and the other man raises her skirts and lays bare a glorious bottom; she turns and twists in every direction.

The other robber after feeling her bosoms, finally draws them out and admires them, and taking an enormous prick out of his trousers, rubs it gently between her snow-white legs.

At last she quiets down and her struggles cease. The other robber too, draws out his prick and placing it first in her arse, at last presents it at the entrance of her handsome portico.

The beauty again resists, but she allows him to introduce the haughty head of his prick between the shuddering lips of her cunt. His need must have been great, for he had scarcely given two or three shoves before he spends.

At this, the other robber raises her skirts and putting her in the desired position, enters also by the front. The poor traveller overwhelmed them both with insults and renewed her struggles, but now the tall fellow inserted his instrument, and the more she wriggled and twisted, the more she excited him. He holds her two hands in one of his and applies his mouth to hers.

He kisses her beautiful titties and discharges at the very moment that she spits into his face. It is only after satisfying themselves five or six times apiece that they tie her to a tree and leave her at the mercy of other brigands, or some passerby.

Scarcely have they disappeared when a monk passes by. He crosses himself as he perceives the handsome cunt so well exposed. The woman implores him to untie her and he does so, when she relates her story to him. She is about thirty-five years old and from her story he learns that she is the Lady Superior of a convent not far distant, but she does not give its name.

She had donned a costume to preserve her identity while on a visit. The coach was stopped by two brigands, and she was made to descend. Being the only woman in it, they ordered the driver to continue his journey and leave her with them. No one, not a single man had the courage to interfere, but allowed the robbers to drag her to the woods.

As the Abbess finished her story, her eyes assumed a strange look. The nudity which she was unable to cover was beautiful in the extreme, so dimpled and so white. The monk does not dare look at her but she looks at him and I soon perceive that this poor St Anthony is having a rude trial to support.

With no thought but of the passion which has been awakened by the repeated assaults of the brigands, the Lady Superior suddenly throws herself on the monk, seizes his enormous prick, which would have filled her two hands, and quickly raising his robe, straddles him, planting his big tool in her burning orifice before the monk can interfere.

She does all the work, holds the instrument in one hand and supports herself with the other resting on the grass. She belabours him with her lower pouting lips in great style and at last, spends, minipulating the enormous prick much as the instrument she hides so carefully in the convent, and uses every night when going to bed.

The monk supports the attack admirably; his prick is still as stiff at the moment when the Abbess writhes in the act of spending, as at the beginning of the amorous battle. She spends, but is just warmed up to thorough lasciviousness. She also desires to satisfy him and not knowing what to do, her slit being bruised and sore, she presents to him her big arse and allows him to satisfy himself.

He runs his long prick against her arse cheeks while the skin rises and falls on the extremity. Finally, the Lady Superior gives a movement or two of her backside and an enormous jet spurts out.

CHAPTER SEVEN

"How long have I been asleep?" is the first question I ask the Count, as he enters my room.

"Thirty-six hours," he says, "or at least so says Ivan, for I have slept just as long myself. My dear Monsieur Dormeuil, I wished you to become acquainted with the strange sensations and visions caused by hashish!"

This explained the fanciful dreams I had had. I remained a few days longer with the Count and then returned to Paris to resume my old habits.

I reached my apartment at ten o'clock and surprised Jean in conversation with a chambermaid living in the neighbourhood. I was able to approach them without being heard. She was just showing the boob how to do it.

"Great idiot! Wait until I rub that tool of yours," said she, and began rubbing his prick and shaking it, too. "Take my titties, John dear. Not that way, you hurt me. There, that's it. Now tickle the nipples. You see, you begin to grow stiffer. Put your hand under my skirt—there—feel my leg. Wait, you are too rough; you hurt me with your big fingers; now there, what do you feel? Is it wet? Now put your finger in—not there, you are too far down. How stupid you are. I tell you, that is my arsehole. Ah, now you are stiff as a Grenadier. Now is the time—what are you doing—that is the right place, but you are hurting me; take your hand away and you will see."

She takes his prick and puts it between her thighs. "There—shove, John—not so hard—don't you see you keep slipping. There it is—now push. Easy at first—wait, I will get it in myself!" And at last she gets it into her cunt.

The amorous combat commences and lasts for some time. Several times she is about to spend but the idiot allowed his prick to slip out. Evidently it is his first experience and that is why she displays so much patience. Finally he spends, and I hear him say to her, "I did not feel anything much, did you?"

"Yes, I did, it was ever so good; you are a ninny. Do you want to have another one?"

But I thought that another one would be too long, so I began to cough and called Jean as loudly as I could. I heard a rustle of skirts and then Jean appeared, as red as a poppy.

He was very glad to see me back and for that matter, I was not sorry to be at home again.

I soon pay my respects to my terrible neighbour and am delighted with my reception as I found her quite improved in manner. She has changed her style of dressing her hair and looks much younger. She wears a close fitting dress which displays her still slender form to advantage.

Our conversation becomes quite animated. She asks me a thousand questions.

I next go to our restaurant and next to Mademoiselle Hortense whose little cunt I explore of course, since it is part of my Thursday programme. My correspondence is scant and uninteresting. I go to see Madame X—, but I do not return there in the evening, for I feel the effects of the days spent at Poissy.

The next morning I receive a letter from the Count announcing his intention to start for Russia.

Wanda desires him to take the trip, so he will go. He sends his compliments to me.

This departure grieves me; I have really taken a liking to this peculiar individual, and for some days I feel out of sorts. I spend a great deal of my time in the company of Madame Benoit and find her decidely more interesting than formerly.

Two weeks have elapsed; I only go to see Madame X—at intervals, and I have not purchased any more gloves. I lie in bed and think of the past, and have day dreams. I no longer have the same love for women. I do not feel the same regard of gratifying my passions. Another fortnight passes away and brings me tidings from the Count.

I am more and more in Madame Benoit's company and . . . shall I acknowledge it? I have made a proposition of marriage to her.

Who would have thought that one day I would be a husband and Madame Benoit my wife?

Now and then I kiss the lips of my betrothed and I dare not attempt a liberty, but tomorrow night I shall have the plump body of my wife entwined in my arms in this bed or hers, whichever she may like better.

The wedding takes place as arranged. It is midnight, and all the guests have retired. The women have kissed the bride and whispered to their hearts' content.

Naturally, Madame Dormeuil blushes lightly every time she meets my eyes, which becomes her very much. I take her on my knees and try to assist her to take off her waist. She will not allow that.

"Stop! I beg of you," she exclaims.

I take a kiss, then another, a third . . . a great many. However at last I find myself in my own room. She would not grant me the conjugal bed tonight. She denied me so charmingly that I could not insist. I go to bed feeling cross and out of humour. Several times during the night I feel like forcing the other door that separates the cruel one from me. But I am afraid of the noise and the scandal.

We spend the next day in the suburbs of Paris. The weather is so beautiful that we decided to go to the country. My wife is quite lively and eats and drinks with appetite.

We return at nine o'clock and as I take off her shoes, I take the liberty of examining the commencement of round, well turned leg. Madame Dormeuil will not shut the door in my face tonight! We have a lengthy discussion on that point, but she will do her duty as a wife. She says that I am to be forbidden the sight of her disrobing, so I am banished temporarily to my own apartment. Twice have I gone to the door but have not been admitted. At last I am able to turn the knob. The lamp on the table is turned very low and the room is so dark that I can scarcely distinguish the bed, the curtains of which are drawn.

It does not take me long to undress, then I slip in between the sheets where a slight warmth alone betrays her presence. I wait a few minutes, but my wife does not show any intention of beginning a conversation.

"Dearest!" I venture to say then: "Gertrude! Gertrude!"

Perhaps she is asleep, and I touch her gently on the back. At the contact of my finger she doubles herself up and draws close to the wall, but I become bolder and in my title of husband, put my arm about her waist, and draw her to me. I forcibly turn her face to mine and impress a burning kiss upon her lips.

I feel her big bosoms and press them close to me; I turn her quickly in my arms, but she begs me to let her sleep. It appears so ridiculous to her to have me in her bed, she has become so accustomed to consider me as a friend, as a brother, and so on. As she speaks, she hides her head in my bosom. I cannot stand it any longer. Little by little I have raised her chemise.

I pass my hand over her legs, her large bottom, and press it gently. Then I suddenly thrust one leg between her thighs, explore her legs, the knees, then further up. As I feel the luxuriant hair against my leg, I grasp her pouting pussy, then again I feel her bosoms. They fill my hands, firm yet so soft. Now my hand descends to her great cunt. What a beauty she has! Surely she must feel my prick; it is like a great club against her body.

"Anatole, I beg of you, not tonight, tomorrow night if you like!"

"No, my darling, tonight, now!" I say passionately and I succeed but not without some difficulty in getting between her legs; then I immediately try to place my tool at the entrance of her big pussy. On pressing a little, I enter with ease. I give a vigorous shove and I am there! I begin to rub softly and put one hand under her bottom. It does not take her long to respond.

"Anatole, kiss me," she murmurs. Presently I kiss her again, her tongue responds to mine and her arse moves, keeping time as I enter and leave the little grotto of love. I kiss her voluptuous bosom and I move still faster.

"Anatole, how good it is. Not so fast! Ah! Ah! Ah! A little faster now. Faster!! It is so delightful. Ah-h-h-h!!"

And now her big bottom goes like a steam engine and she squeezes my tool and plays with my balls. I take good care not to stop her. She is coming! I feel it—there it is!

"Anatole, I am coming, my darling! Oh, I love you, my husband, my darling!" and her great bottom falls heavily on my hands. We spend once, then spend again, and I am still ready to spend the third time.

After three successive assaults, we go to sleep in each other's arms, but before closing my eyes I calculate how many years my wife had to remain without having relations with a man and admit that fate is indeed hard on a woman.

The next day, when I look at Madame Dormeuil I remember my reflection of the night before and I give her a hearty kiss without telling her why. Things go on pretty much the same after the first night, but without any struggle on her part.

I had been happy in my new existence for a month, when I received a letter from Count Alexis.

In order to give you an idea of the effect it had on me, I will reproduce it.

My dear Dormeuil,

My dear friend, you must either have thought I had forgotten you or that I was dead. My silence was caused by much work and great uncertainty of mind.

Do you remember Wanda? She is here with me. I was sick and she took care of me with wonderful devotion. Many admirers, young, rich and titled, have asked for her hand in marriage. She refused them all and seems happy only by my side. Before so much devotion, I, the high-lived, have succumbed. My heart has spoken; I am going to marry Wanda.

According to the French custom, before my marriage, I intend to give an entertainment to all my friends. It will be my last bachelor's dinner and I cordially invite you to attend. My next letter will give you the date. I shall count upon you and we will be sure to have a good time.

By the way, I have a confidence to make to you. You remember when I visited Madame Benoit, your terrible neighbour. When I told her I was sent by you, I found her in a bad humour. One of my little jokes at last, however, made her smile, then laugh heartily.

Unintentionally, a naughty word or two would creep into the conversation, and I remember that she made me repeat them. Her hearing was not so very good perhaps; to be frank with you, I took a few liberties which were not badly received, and one thing which you will certainly not believe, my dear Dormeuil, is that Madame Benoit's skin is very soft and that her bosoms are magnificently firm.

Once warmed up by the coquetry of your neighbour, I raised her skirts and presented you-know-what, at the entrance of her retreat.

Plenty of beautifully curling hairs and big thighs, on my word!

You doubt the fact I am sure, and think me insane, but it is true for all that; I shall always remember that glorious mount. It was one of the best I ever had.

Your neighbour fucks well; I should never have dreamed of such a thing, and it was in your interest that I carried matters so far. That is undoubtedly the reason of your charming reception on your return; now good luck to you; use this little confidence as you please. Try it yourself; she is not as terrible as she looks. Let me hear from you pretty soon. I expect your visit shortly.

With cordial good wishes, I am your friend,
ALEXIS.

Who would have thought such a thing! Oh, Madame Benoit, the prude. But I reasoned with myself. After all, Madame Benoit was free at that time to do as she pleased and I was a fool.

A week ago, I myself broke our marriage vows. I received a letter, giving me a rendezvous at 37 Rue de l'Ecoille. It was Miss Anderson, whom Count Alexis had met at Naples. She was still in love with him and asked me news of him. I have revenged myself on the Count with this young English girl.

I pressed her so hard that I laid her on the bed, and, raising her skirts, introduced my tool into her reception room before she had time to refuse. She worked well and vigorously, and I soon gave her a reserve of sperm which I had saved up, as my wife was angry with me.

She is a very loving and lovely thing, this little auburn-haired girl. She really spends with the finesse of art. I see her often and she has promised to stay here another month.

I have abandoned the idea of going to Russia,

neither will I be angry with Gertrude, who is quite
enough—more than enough for me now!

STAR BOOKS ADULT READS

FICTION

BEATRICE	Anonymous	£2.25*
EVELINE	Anonymous	£2.25*
MORE EVELINE	Anonymous	£2.25*
FRANK & I	Anonymous	£2.25*
A MAN WITH A MAID	Anonymous	£2.25*
A MAN WITH A MAID 2	Anonymous	£2.25*
A MAN WITH A MAID 3	Anonymous	£2.25*
OH WICKED COUNTRY	Anonymous	£2.25*
ROMANCE OF LUST VOL 1	Anonymous	£2.25*
ROMANCE OF LUST VOL 2	Anonymous	£2.25*
SURBURBAN SOULS VOL 1	Anonymous	£2.25*
SURBURBAN SOULS VOL 2	Anonymous	£2.25*
DELTA OF VENUS	Anais Nin	£1.60*
LITTLE BIRDS	Anais Nin	£1.60*
PLAISIR D'AMOUR	A.M.Villefranche	£2.25
JOIE D'AMOUR	A.M.Villefranche	£2.25

STAR BOOKS ADULT READS

FICTION

ADVENTURES OF A SCHOOLBOY	Anonymous	£2.25
AUTOBIOGRAPHY OF A FLEA	Anonymous	£2.25*
MEMOIRES OF DOLLY MORTEN	Anonymous	£2.25
LAURA MIDDLETON	Anonymous	£2.25
THREE TIMES A WOMAN	Anonymous	£2.25*
THE BOUDOIR	Anonymous	£2.25*
THE LUSTFUL TURK	Anonymous	£2.25*
MAUDIE	Anonymous	£2.25*
RANDIANA	Anonymous	£2.25*
ROSA FIELDING	Anonymous	£2.25*
JOY	Joy Laurey	£2.25
JOY AND JOAN	Joy Laurey	£2.25
INSTRUMENT OF PLEASURE	Celeste Piano	£2.25
OPUS PISTORUM	Henry Miller	£2.25*

STAR Books are obtainable from many booksellers and newsagents. If you have any difficulty tick the titles you want and fill in the form below.

_____

Name _____

Address _____ _____

_____

Send to: Star Books Cash Sales, P.O. Box 11, Falmouth, Cornwall, TR10 9EN.

Please send a cheque or postal order to the value of the cover price plus:
UK: 55p for the first book, 22p for the second book and 14p for each additional book ordered to the maximum charge of £1.75.

BFPO and EIRE: 55p for the first book, 22p for the second book, 14p per copy for the next 7 books, thereafter 8p per book.

OVERSEAS: £1.00 for the first book and 25p per copy for each additional book.

While every effort is made to keep prices low, it is sometimes necessary to increase prices at short notice. Star Books reserve the right to show new retail prices on covers which may differ from those advertised in the text or elsewhere.

NOT FOR SALE IN CANADA

STAR BOOKS ADULT READS

FICTION

EROTICON	Anonymous	£2.25
LASCIVIOUS SCENES	Anonymous	£2.25*
PARISIAN FROLICS	Anonymous	£2.25
PLEASURE BOUND AFLOAT	Anonymous	£2.25
PLEASURE BOUND ASHORE	Anonymous	£2.25
THE FIESTA LETTERS	Fiesta	£2.50
INDISCREET MEMOIRES	Alain Dorval	£2.25
NYMPH IN PARIS	Galia S	£2.25
LAURE-ANNE	Laure-Anne	£2.25
PLEASURES OF LOVING	Maren Sell(ed)	£2.25
A LETTER FROM MY FATHER	Page Smith	£2.25
A LETTER FROM MY FATHER 2	Page Smith	£2.25
BEACH OF PASSION	Donald Bowie	£1.95

STAR Books are obtainable from many booksellers and newsagents. If you have any difficulty tick the titles you want and fill in the form below.

Name _____

Address _____

_____

Send to: Star Books Cash Sales, P.O. Box 11, Falmouth, Cornwall, TR10 9EN.

Please send a cheque or postal order to the value of the cover price plus:
UK: 55p for the first book, 22p for the second book and 14p for each additional book ordered to the maximum charge of £1.75.

BFPO and EIRE: 55p for the first book, 22p for the second book, 14p per copy for the next 7 books, thereafter 8p per book.

OVERSEAS: £1.00 for the first book and 25p per copy for each additional book.

While every effort is made to keep prices low, it is sometimes necessary to increase prices at short notice. Star Books reserve the right to show new retail prices on covers which may differ from those advertised in the text or elsewhere.

*NOT FOR SALE IN CANADA